Take
The
Helm

Susan Larned Womble

Published by Page Pond Press

Published by Page Pond Press
www.pagepondpress.com

Inquiries should be addressed to: Page Pond Press at www.pagepondpress.com
email: pagepondpress1@gmail.com

ISBN: 0991397770
ISBN-13: 978-0-9913977-7-8

First Edition

Printed in the United States of America
Copyright © 2014 Susan Larned Womble

All rights reserved.

ISBN: 0991397770
ISBN-13: 978-0-9913977-7-8

DEDICATION

For my husband, Gregg

My partner for all the good stuff
Here's to many more adventures!!

Take the Helm

Susan Larned Womble

Published by Page Pond Press

ACKNOWLEDGMENTS

I would like to acknowledge the support of my family, Gregg, Thomas, Amanda, Harper, my dad, Tommy, and sister, Judi. I would also like to thank my writing critique group; Hannah Mahler, Rhett DeVane, Peggy Kassess, and Donna Meredith. They help with every aspect of the writing process and keep me on track. I would also like to thank my St. George retreat writing buddies, especially our fearless leader, Adrian Fogelin and our organizer, Perky Granger for all of their guidance and fun times every year. First drafts are always at the beach retreat. Special shout out to Paula Kiger, editor extraordinaire. I would also like to thank the teachers of Hohenfels, Germany along with the people of Bavaria and Europe for the wonderful experience of learning about their culture as I travelled throughout Europe.

This is a special shout out to my sister, Judi. You have been my forever friend. You have known me longer than anyone else besides Dad. I can't begin to tell you how your positive ways and unwavering support throughout the years has enriched my life. Our connection has added sprinkles and glitter and every color in the universe to my existence. You were my first friend and I just wanted to publically acknowledge how much you mean to me. I love you Judi.

Chapter 1

Slavery. Human trafficking. It's strong and alive here in my world. A world controlled by royals who only care about power and who think it's acceptable to own and to buy and sell other human beings. If those were the only things wrong with this world, we might stand a chance, but there is so much more.

Perched at the top of the abandoned Ferris wheel, I conduct my daily exercise. Twelve children ranging in age from six to thirteen scale the monster, swinging from one end to the other. Each child brandishes a stick, our substitute for weapons. I count off the steps, one two, three...Only a few missed beats, no hesitation. We're improving. An army of children. How sad!

We've practiced this next drill a zillion times, but this time Mike, the oldest, slips and bullets from the high rusty beam of the Ferris wheel. A throaty scream slashes through the air. I'm not sure who owns the piercing shriek, but a thud ends it.

A pang of responsibility shoots through my heart, as I fight my urge to go to Mike. I have to follow the contingency plan, which means waiting for Colt. Today, it's Colt's job to be the medic. I can't help Mike. I have to make sure the other eleven on the metal giant get down safely. Been lucky about injuries, a miracle since we live on an isolated farm with twenty or so people who are training for a war that may or may not happen.

Out of the corner of my eye, I see Colt bolt to the crumpled boy. "Paisley, I got him," Colt yells. "Bring the rest down."

Scaling the prongs of the Ferris wheel is like walking for me now. I've done it so many times. I bark orders to my subordinates and they plunge downward in a manner that replicates a fly lighting for a second then fluttering to the next point. A slip of a hand and a few narrow escapes make the descent anything but ordinary. They are improving, but not perfect yet. After all, they're only children.

They complete their task with no mishaps. As the last trainee safely hits the ground, the edges of my mouth curve and an unintentional proud smile grazes my face before I force its disappearance. I stiffen and say, "That will be all for today. Go get some food and I'll see you in the morning."

My orders are not immediately followed. They mill around and a couple march over towards Colt.

"What about Mike?" Amanda brushes past me to the crumpled boy in front of her. She reaches for his hand. "Are you okay?" She drops to her knees. "Is it your leg?"

Colt presses on parts of Mike's leg. When he reaches the calf area, Mike grimaces in pain. "Ouch! Might be broken," Mike groans out an answer to Amanda, "but don't worry I'll be fine." He turns his head toward the others. "Go ahead with them. They'll patch me up and I'll be back at the camp in a few minutes."

Amanda reluctantly joins the others. Colt retrieves a piece of wood and splints Mike's leg. Colt and I have to be the soldier, medic, parent, teacher, trainer, or whatever the situation calls for. We know we have to start teaching the recruits to fend for themselves. Colt and I won't be around forever.

Our small group cares about one another too much. That will probably be our downfall. We can't stay in our protected corner of the world forever. We have to join the fight. It's our mission. What a joke! Don't even know exactly what that is. Our world? An epic mess up. Colt and I are actually under house arrest, or I guess farm arrest. We're not supposed to leave for any reason.

"Don't worry." Colt wraps his arm around my shoulder. "I patched him up. He'll be ready in a week to continue training. At least it wasn't broken."

A pang shoots through me. I slap his arm away. "How do you know that? You're not a doctor." It's not like me to be so curt. I know I'm missing Gretel, my sister. She was the doctor or as close to being a doctor as she could be with no formal schooling. She would know exactly what to do. One of the big reasons I must escape this farm is to find her.

When we arrived a month ago, we were a group of thirty-one. Sixteen of us range in age from eight to seventeen. The rest are older and frail, encumbered by disabilities and injuries. We've lost nine of our oldsters since then, and are in danger of losing two more. Now our group numbers only twenty-two. The losses have been disheartening. At first, Colt and I only trained with the older children. Now, no choice. We must prepare those of us who are healthy and strong even if they are only eight years old.

"We can't fight or teach them to fight if we don't show a united front." Colt plants his feet directly in my path and forces me to stop. "If we expect to win this war and change the world then you and I need to work together. Stop whining."

I shove him. "What are you talking about? How can we leave the children alone? We can't win. They can't even scale a Ferris wheel that's not moving without misses. It's hopeless."

"They're not alone." He motions toward the barn.

I nod. "I know the adults are there, but they need more help than the children. Our plan seemed so solid before, but now I'm not so sure."

"Paisley, it's not hopeless. Something is going to happen, and when it does you'll see why all this training was the right thing."

Does he really believe what he is saying? Maybe he'll understand sarcasm. I keep walking. "Sure, it's the right thing. We'll leave the children. They'll get stronger when we go." I wave my hands around, "Who knows? Maybe Mom and Gretel will escape. The Consortium of the World will decide democracy is the best path and put the ambassador in charge." I step in front of him and stop. "Who is dreaming now? It sure isn't me, Colt. Wake up!" I turn around and face him with my hands thrust firmly upon my hips. "I know we planned to leave soon, but how can we?"

I turn on my heel and Colt follows behind mumbling, "It'll work out, have faith."

I struggle to hold back the tears as I throw open the front door of the two-room shack that I have called home for as long as I can remember. Home? Home is where your family lives. This is not home now. This empty shell houses Colt, twenty misfits, and me. People who were once deemed unfit to live to the point that they were labeled Undesirables because of their disabilities, flaws, or lack of loved ones with the means to take care of them. This world—messed up.

"We should have information from the outside soon." Colt follows me and stands in the doorway. "I sent Thomas on a mission to locate a newspaper so we can find out what's been going on, and maybe the location of the ship your family is on. I hope he makes it back soon." He sighs and looks up at the ceiling. "Wouldn't it be great if he brought us good news?"

"The eternal optimist." I couldn't help but love Colt. He had been like a brother to me during one of the worst times of my life. We almost died together and now we work together in charge of our misfit army.

He smiles. "Always." He squints. "Someone's coming from the woods."

"He's back. Thomas is back!" Mike yells from the yard.

Colt and I rush through the door and see Thomas falling

to his knees. His clothes are ripped and he is covered in mud. He shakes as he pulls out a wadded-up paper from his pocket.

Colt lifts the papers carefully from Thomas' clutched hand. I grab a jug of water. Thomas jerks it from my hand and greedily chugs it. The commotion brings the rest of our drill group in and they crowd around us.

Colt and I sit on the ground beside Thomas. News from the outside world. But is it news that we want?

Colt asks, "Is it good news or bad news?"

Thomas jerks the jug down, water dripping from his chin. "Not good, not good at all."

Chapter 2

"What kind of bad news?" I ask as Thomas drinks again. My mind wanders to every kind of horrible news I can imagine. What if the ship sank and my family drowned? What if the ambassador was killed? Goose bumps arise as I think of the worst of all, what if the virus that wiped out millions and forced a twelve-year quarantine has returned?

Thomas releases the jug. "He's losing. The ambassador is losing." He pokes at the print that Colt is holding.

"Let me see." I pull part of an article from Colt's hand. The two of us silently read for the next few minutes as the rest of the group welcomes Thomas back.

Thomas is right. It's not good news, but do we really need to tell everyone? We've had so many setbacks and deaths, I worry that this might deflate our group. It's sad to me that Thomas is only nine and is already privy to the unfairness of this world. That I can't change. But we can control this bad news. I lean over to share my thoughts and hesitations with Colt.

Amanda, not one to stay in the background long, scoots in beside me. "What's it say?"

"Nothing interesting." I shuffle the article to the side.

"It's time for you to rest now. We have an early practice tomorrow. You need your sleep."

Amanda stands up and stomps her foot, knocking dirt all over me. "You're not telling us! You're keeping it from us. We demand to know!"

I stand up and hug her. "Of course, you should all know. Colt and I haven't had a chance to read everything. We might tell you something that's not true. Please, give us time to look through everything. We won't keep anything from you." I hold Amanda's chin in my hand and gaze into her eyes. "I promise." I have become such a good liar that I scare myself sometimes. But, it works.

The children reluctantly make their way to their assigned sleeping quarters, makeshift tents of sheets. In a few more minutes, it's quiet once again.

"Mike needs to stay in the house until his leg heals, and—" Colt shoots a knowing glance my way and then back to Thomas before continuing. "Thomas, move to the house until you gain your strength back. Can you both make it on your own?"

Mike hops on one leg toward the door and stops to study Thomas's face. He then looks at Colt and me. "You can fool them, but I know there's something in that paper that you don't want the rest to know. Tell me. I'm almost grown. I'm thirteen." Mike stands, jutting his chin out defiantly and crossing his arms.

Thomas nods. "He's right. He's old enough."

This secret, we can't keep. At least not from these two. Thomas knows, and he will tell Mike. I walk toward the Ferris wheel. I dread this conversation. I know that it's time for Colt and me to go. We should tell them. We should tell every one of them tonight, the oldsters too. My shoulders droop as I announce, "I'll gather the rest."

Hiking through my farm to the barn housing the oldsters is surreal. No more harvesting our farm for the Mercs, hiding from them, or worrying about being an Uncounted. My worries now are of the global kind. The battle for control is immense and in my mind unwinnable. Why are we trying?

Simple, we must.

"Heather?" I spy one of the women fretting about outside the barn, portioning our dinner for the night. "Help me gather the rest. We need to talk." I help her divvy up stalks of corn. "Are Joe and Arlas doing any better?"

Heather shakes her head. Entering the barn is like visiting a hospital. Beds contain what's left of the former Undesirables. Bandages cover most of their limbs and the stench of disinfectant and sickness permeates the hay that surrounds them. It would be easier to have the meeting here, but Colt and I had decided long ago to keep the children out of the barn. Too much sadness, too much sickness. It just didn't feel right.

I move a blanket to cover the oldest man, Joe. "We need to have a meeting in the house. We have news that we want to share."

Only four decide to attempt the trek across from the barn to the house. Three women and one man. How can we possibly make a difference with so few? I push the negative thought from my mind. We move at a turtle's pace from the dilapidated barn, dodging the rusted turbines and cars. All reminders of the decades before the virus, before the royals, before the Consortium of the World, before the struggle for democracy, before human trafficking was the norm.

Inside the house, we take our places around the room on the threadbare sofa, the rundown chairs, and decaying stools.

"What's the news?" The man, Jack, asks.

I feel my shoulders drop.

Jack takes in a deep breath. "That bad, huh?"

I don't answer, but spread the articles on the chipped coffee table that sits on blocks. Its legs rotted off long ago. "There is some good news; others are attempting to do what we are doing so we're not alone."

Jack asks, "How would we know that? I thought the media was controlled by the royals."

I nod. "Unfortunately you are right, it still is. But newspapers report problems. We think this is the handwork of the resistance. There are articles about them throughout the newspaper. They destroy meeting places."

"How do they destroy them?" asks Gina, a pretty older woman with a mangled arm.

"Some use explosives," Colt answers, "but mostly by axing out support beams and causing the structures to collapse. It's easy to do with most buildings being in such disrepair."

Gina breathes out. "Good, I didn't want our children to go into places where bombs were set. I know it's dangerous work, but –" She stops for a moment. "I'm just glad we're not planning on going into bomb-riddled places."

I add, "The children aren't going at all." I stop for a minute. I might have said too much. I explain, "I mean they still have to train."

Jack lets out another exasperated sigh. "Let them finish. I want to hear the news."

I report. "There are many factions of unrest, but we are all spread out. This article is about the ambassador's trip. He has completed his voyage around Europe on the "Queen Nalani" ship and—" My voice cracks, "—is planning on traveling on the same ship to America in two weeks."

Jane, a rotund woman, scoots over to me and slips her arm around my shoulder. "Aren't your mom and sister on that ship?"

"Yes."

"That's why we called you together," Colt interrupts. "We need to figure out what to do next."

"We need to join with the other groups." Mike sits up, rubbing his splinted leg. "The only way that we defeat them is to have a bigger army, one that can make a difference."

A nine-year-old boy, Beau, slips out from his hiding place in a closet. "I agree with Mike. We're too few, like fleas on a lion. We need to join the others."

Mike smiles. "And be like a club knocking that lion's head off."

Beau laughs and shoves his fist in the air. "Yes!"

How can these children speak with such maturity? They

have grown up too fast. Here is a nine-year old talking with wisdom far beyond his years. Children. Children must be included in any plan. Why? Because they have to soldier the army. We have to be realistic. We can't leave them out.

I'm not sure how long the others, the old ones, will survive. Deemed as Undesirable because of their flaws, their years have been cut short because we have no usable medicines to make them better or any real food to make them stronger. They brought the children here to give them a fighting chance at survival, but in doing so, they signed their own death warrants. It's part of what makes the Uncounteds and Undesirables so strong, their sense of duty and sacrifice. Traits that have eluded most of the Mercs and royals. So unfair!

"We need a plan of action," I say. "Mike's right. We need to search others out." I nod quickly at Colt and scan the rest of the room. "Gina and Heather and the rest of you need to stay here on the farm. You are too weak to leave." They open their mouths in what I can only surmise will be a protest so I cut them off, "The children need you. You need to take care of Joe and Arlas. It's the only way."

Gina drops her head. "I guess we really are still Undesirable."

My face burns with anger at the mention of that word. "You are not Undesirables! None of you ever were!" I stop and catch my breath.

Colt finishes my thought, something we do now. "It's important that we know those left behind on the farm have the best care. We have to take into account physical limitations."

"Plus we plan on kicking butt and coming back with news of a better world. A world of freedom. Everyone free, not just the rich." I gain calmness as I speak.

"Everyone needs to be in on this decision," announces Thomas as he heads for the door. "I'm going to get the others from the barn." He disappears into the night.

"We have to get on that ship," I whisper to Colt. "Mom and Gretel are on that ship."

Colt's eyes go dreamy for a moment. I'm sure it's at the thought of seeing Gretel. Colt's in love with my sister. I guess if

I really thought about it, Colt will probably be my brother one day. Only problem, my sister and my mom think we're dead. My mind conjures up Riley. Guess he thinks I'm dead. It makes me happy to think about him being on that ship too.

"We need a plan." Colt hides his mouth as he talks. "We can't leave those young ones here without us unless we know they'll be safe. I don't know how long the adults can hang on."

He's right. I guess if we're honest about it, we're part of the young ones. Colt's turning eighteen soon and I'm only fifteen. I feel grown-up. Maybe we skipped our childhoods. I turn my back to the group and speak softly to Colt. "What do you take me for? I'm not heartless. I know we have to make sure they're all right. I don't plan to leave anyone in harm's way. Don't worry. We'll figure it out."

"With a real plan?" He smiles, still voicing low, "Or letting it happen? You're better when you just luck into things."

I laugh. Laughter is so scarce here. I like it when something is funny even if it's only for a fleeting moment. It's hard not to melt into it, but right now, we need to be serious. The adults need both my and Colt's care. We know we are the caretakers. Some of the children even call me *Mom*. I'm fifteen, but I still feel like a mother hen, a responsible mother hen.

Half an hour later, our entire group crowds into my house. We occupy every free space in the room.

Colt clears his throat. "I think we should let Thomas speak about what is going on outside this farm. After all, he did make it there and back."

Thomas stands and thrusts his hands in his pockets. One hand pushes through the fabric lining. Thomas's eyes widen and he shifts uncomfortably before he attempts to use his other hand to free the stuck hand to no avail. The more he jerks, the more the hand disappears into the lining leaving him standing crooked and totally flustered. The more he moves, the more ridiculous he looks. Beau laughs. Thomas turns red and Mike tries so hard to hold a laugh that he moves his leg, hurting it until he yelps in pain. A couple of the women rush to help Thomas right his jacket.

If I don't do something, no one is going to take him seriously. I decide to rescue him, something I do a lot of nowadays.

"Thomas, we'll hear from you in a moment." I fold my hands together in front of my chest, like I saw a speaker do once in a picture. That gesture made me want to hear what she was going to say. I hope it has the same effect here.

The room quiets down. So far, so good. I talk in a low, whispery voice. "We have a couple of problems. One, we need to work with a bigger group and unless there are some people hidden in the forest that we don't know about then this—" I wave my hands around. "—is all we got."

"What about the families that you and Colt saved from the other farms?" Thomas pipes in. "We've heard those stories over and over. Where are they?"

He has a point. We liberated a large group of farm families after the Mercs took over their farms. Saved them from human trafficking. Colt's family was among them, but unfortunately, we've lost touch with them.

They were not where they were supposed to be and we have no way of tracking them. Maybe we shouldn't have left it that way, but we wanted them to be safe. We can only hope that we will run into them or that democracy will win then everyone will come out of hiding.

On a positive note, the fact that we couldn't find them means the Mercs won't be able to either. Patience. It's easier to talk about than actually do.

"Good point, Thomas." Colt scoots closer to me. "We don't know where they ended up. They might be right around the corner. They might have been caught or they may have relocated elsewhere. We can't wait on them. We've been here a month and—"

"I want to wait!" Gina yells out. "We need them and—what did you say? There might be as many as fifty?"

Joe struggles to hold his hand up. "Me and Arlas ain't gonna be no help. I say we wait on the others."

Thomas jumps up and down. "I didn't say *to wait*. I just wondered where they are." He sits back down with a thump.

14

"Sorry I brought it up." He looks at Colt. "Colt, what's your plan?"

Colt doesn't move or comment.

Can't wait any longer. I shout, hands on my hips, "Listen, we have three major problems. One, we have too small of a group. Two, the only healthy people are children." I stop for a minute and wave my hand toward Joe and Arlas. "No offense, but we've got to do something."

"Why?" Amanda rubs her eyes.

I must have asked that question a thousand times when my mother homeschooled us. Now it just irks me. How can I answer why about a question or plan of action that I'm not sure about myself? I lie, that's what I do and hope for the best.

I answer like my mom always did. "Just because." Amanda doesn't ask another question so I continue, "Number three is that my mom and Gretel are on that ship and that ship is going to America in a couple of weeks."

Thomas asks, "Why does that matter?"

"Because I'm leaving to find some groups for us to join. While I'm gone, *you* still need to train. You need to take charge of yourselves. You need to have a concrete daily plan for survival and you need to stick to it. You need to do all of that because *I'm* going to search for that ship and try to free Mom and Gretel.

And if I don't succeed," I pause and take a deep breath, "I'm going to America and I won't be back for a very long time."

Chapter 3

T he reaction and noise accompanying it is deafening. Our entire group sits on the floor and in various chairs facing each other. There is not much space in between, but everyone still seems to feel the need to speak loudly. Maybe it's because they think no one will listen. It's understandable. They have been ignored for most of their lives, labeled and cast aside as Uncounteds or Undesirables. Sadly now with so many voices speaking all at once, *no one* is being understood.

Finally, Colt stands up and holds his hands up demanding to be heard. He shouts, "Paisley will have company!" The room quiets. Colt shoves his shoulder into mine. "I'm going with her."

"Have you both lost your mind?" Gina stands and wags her finger as she speaks. "You can't leave. You're under house arrest. If they catch you, they'll execute you."

"For Mom and Gretel, I'm willing to take the chance." I grab Gina's wiggling finger. "I know you mean well, but to be honest I don't want to live this way. Not being able to go anywhere. The first part of my life I was imprisoned by the quarantine because of the virus. The next part of my life I'm going to be free or die trying to be free."

Arlas is unable to stand so he shifts on the couch, and puts his thoughts in the conversation. "We were *all* quarantined."

"That's true and now we're searching for a way to be free." I nod at him as I speak. "I don't want anyone to think I don't realize what you've been through, but you've got to understand it's my family. My plan is to not only save them, I want to save everyone." I point to the children. "That's what all of this has been about. All this training, every day we've been working toward our freedom."

Mike jumps up from his spot on the rug, hops on his good leg, and shouts, "If you leave, who's in charge?"

"I'm looking at the new army leader." Colt throws an arm around Mike. "You're ready. With you training the younger ones and Thomas running reconnaissance, your group will be strong. Heck, with your fire and determination, you might just be unstoppable."

Mike smiles, pulls Thomas to his feet, and the two stand shoulder to chest since Mike is taller. "We *are* a pretty good team."

"You're a *great* team." I smile at them. "You don't really need us anymore." I say it, but I'm not sure if it's true. I hope it's true, but they must believe that they can make it on their own. If they believe it, then maybe they can do it without us. I'm not sure if I'm making this argument because I believe it or because I don't want to feel the guilt that I feel now. Either way, we have to leave them in charge of themselves. It's the only choice.

Jane sits quietly on the tattered couch and shakes her head. "But we do need you. I am fearful about what will happen when you go."

I plop down beside by Jane. "You don't really need us to run the farm. You, Gina, and the others know how to do that. You know how to get the harvest. With fewer of us here, it'll be easier. Less mouths to feed."

"But what happens if the Mercs come back?" Jane chokes out.

I put my arm around her shoulder. "If the Mercs come back, you'll deal with it. Hide. None of you is supposed to be here anyway. The only difference if we were here is that the Mercs could take us to prison. Then none of us would have this chance. We have to seize this opportunity before the Consortium of the World is decided. If democracy doesn't win out, then none of us will be able to do anything about it. It has to happen now."

A tear runs down Jane's face.

I choke. "If you cry, I'll cry." I swallow a sob. "It's time. I have to try to save Mom and Gretel." I grab her hands and squeeze. "I probably won't get another chance. You understand. It's family."

Jane wipes her eyes and nods too. "We're your family too."

I sigh. "Don't you think I realize that? I have to do this. It's what's best for everyone."

Nods around the room signify that all agree.

Colt shakes Mike's hand. "Then it's decided. I never doubted that Paisley would convince you. She can be quite persuasive when she wants to be."

"And I want to be." My smile is shaky. "I *have* to be."

Gina hugs me. "Let's get Joe and Arlas back to their beds."

I shove my shoulder under Joe's arm. He lets out a groan of pain, but quiets after that. Colt and I will discuss when to make our move. But it has to be in the next couple of days or the ship will be gone and then it will be too late.

The next two days are full of last-minute instructions, strenuous drills, and sad good-byes. Unable to sleep the night before we plan to go, I tiptoe out to my Ferris wheel, throw the switch to the lowest speed, and sit in the bottom chair. I want that ride one last time just in case I don't make it back. Moving this slowly, the wheel lulls me to a half-sleep. I don't know why I want to sleep on the Ferris wheel, but I do. I pull out my four-leaf clover bullet that was owned by Riley and roll it in my hand. He fashioned it as a good luck piece. It's brought me luck so far, I hope it can continue. It's easier to keep up with since I put it on a necklace. Riley is on the ship too and the thought of seeing him again excites me. My mind fills with of all the things that can go wrong. It's a struggle to fall asleep.

"Wake up sleepy-head." Colt's voice. He opens the door to the Ferris wheel carriage with a creak. "I've been looking for you in the house. Should have known this is where you'd be. It's time to go. Are you packed?"

I see the sun peeking above the horizon.

"I packed last night." I rub the sleep out of my eyes. "What time is it? Is it morning? I thought I'd never fall asleep last night." I step out of the carriage and look toward the house. "Is anyone awake yet? Should we say a last good-bye?" I stretch my arms over my head. "Did you stop the wheel?"

"Yes. You're full of questions." He pulls at my sleeve. "Did you sleep in your clothes?"

I slap at him and throw on my backpack. "Of course, so I'd be ready just in case you left me. I planned on running after you."

He chuckles a little. "I hate good-byes." He sighs. "It'll be sad. Let's go. No use making a big scene."

I take a longing look at the Ferris wheel. I love that old metal rusty giant. It represents home. But home is people, not an object, home is Gretel and Mom. I turn my back on the wheel and cut my eyes over at Colt. "I don't know about you, but I plan on trying my hardest to make it back to this farm. With Mom and..."

"Gretel." He smiles. I'm positive I know what he's thinking and it makes me blush. We have definitely been together too long.

It's been a while since I've travelled this far off my farm. The snow hasn't fallen yet so the ground is still green. Bavaria is so beautiful this time of year. When my family was together, we were too focused on getting the harvest to enjoy our scenery.

Being locked on the ship for so long made me appreciate nature and our forest. The open sea is nice but it sure doesn't compare to the Bavarian green hills. A few deer gracefully hop in our path giving us a scare. We fear running into the Mercs, the ones who imprisoned us in the first place. Mercs are just in it for the wealth and power. That's something that the royals and Mercs have in common. While the quarantine was in force, no one challenged their authority, but now that the world is slowly waking up, everyone is jockeying for a position of power. The Mercs still murder first and ask questions later. We don't want to be on the receiving end of one of their killing sprees.

The red and yellow foliage paints a spectacular canvas, as if nature is communicating that there is still good in the world. The beauty surrounding me makes me forget everything else for the moment. As breathtaking as this path is, it is a reminder that things and people who are pleasing to the eye get the most attention. I realize that as we pull the wine berries off the most unattractive vines. The beautiful meadows are wonderful to look at it, but they don't feed you. In contrast, the vines in the vineyards are not only unpleasing they also are scratchy and downright ugly, but what do they do? Their berries feed you when you're hungry.

Makes me think of the rich people on the ship who got all of the attention. Everyone caters to them, but do they do anything for anyone else? Do they make a difference in the world? Most of the time, no.

But the less fortunate, the Undesirables and the Uncounteds, they do all of the work. They bring in the harvest that feeds the world. I could drive myself crazy thinking about how the world is not fair, but today Colt and I just need to keep moving.

Getting out of our forest without discovery proves to be a formidable task. We finally decide to go down Dead Man's Row. It's the most disturbing route, but also the less travelled. It's where the Mercs bring their murdered and throw them into a deep ravine. Savages!

"I hear someone. Quick!" I dive into the bushes, yanking Colt beside me.

It's a Merc riding alone dragging a lifeless body behind

his horse. His horse grazes our bush and we have an unencumbered view of the corpse. It's a boy. He couldn't be any older than twelve. A tear escapes my eye and I swallow a gasp.

I want so badly to run over and knock that Merc off his horse. I want to pound him into the ground. The dead body of the child proves this Merc is dangerous. But I can't chance discovery. What could that boy have possibly done that would have warranted death?

The Merc crawls off his horse and ambles slowly back to the lad, like a wolf circling his prey. Prey? His prey is dead. Is he taking pleasure in admiring his work? How sick! He heaves a large knife high over his head. I can't watch.

I hide my eyes for a second before the gore of it draws me back. I let my breath go as I see him whack the rope a few times near the boy's feet. At least he's not mutilating the body. Not yet. I shudder. He pulls the free rope away and walks toward his horse, leaving the youngster in a heap in the middle of the dirt. Like trash.

Colt and I haven't spoken since we hid in the bushes. I glance at him. His horrified expression matches exactly how I feel. There is nothing to be done for the poor dead lad, but still my heart aches.

The Merc takes his time to roll up the rope. My only thought is that he wants to make sure he has it for the next time he plans to murder someone. If we kill this Merc, then he won't be around to slaughter any more innocent boys. I make a slight movement, but Colt's hand pressures my arm. I move again, and he squeezes harder. The more I move the more he presses until my arm goes numb. I look up at him. He shakes his head with a slight move. I know he's right, but it's just so hard not to do anything.

The Merc takes his time collecting the corpse and heaving it over his shoulder. Some blood drops on his boot. He shakes his fists, curses, and slams the boy's dead body down. He stomps the corpse a few times, swearing about how the lad has messed up a perfectly good pair of boots. This boy's life is worth less than a pair of boots. What kind of a person is this?

He lifts the youth up one last time, yanking him over his shoulder and walking to the edge of the ravine. Instead of throwing the body over, he slams it on the edge and kicks the corpse over the side, leaning over to watch the body fall. One thing for sure, the boy's soul is now free. Another thing I know for certain is that this Merc doesn't have a soul.

I'm so horrified that I shift my position. The bush moves. The Merc is on us quickly, slapping me hard in the face. My face stings and I fall backward toward on the ground, struggling to keep my footing. He snatches Colt by the collar. Colt squirms to break free. I grasp at the Merc and scream. He shoves me harder and I slam against a tree. Pain shoots through me, but I go after him again slapping at his arm. He yanks a hunk of my hair with his free hand. I yelp in pain as he jerks me away from Colt. Even with both of us struggling against him, he holds fast. He has a death grip on me and Colt is in a clutch wedged firmly to the Merc's side by the Merc's massive arm. I see Colt struggling, but his arms are locked. Colt's kicking him though. Good for him. Murderers are strong, or at least this murderer is.

"Let us go!" I shriek.

The Merc laughs. "I plan to in just a minute, but you better watch it girlie, that first step is a long one." He laughs again. "Let's get rid of your friend. We don't need him. Plus, he's a little hard to hold onto. Heck, I might keep you around for a bit after he's gone."

The Merc shoves me once more away from him and I crash against a tree, hitting my head. I'm dazed for a moment. He then concentrates his full strength on Colt. He dangles Colt, hanging onto his collar almost choking him over the deep crevasse. "It'll be over quick. Thank you for giving me the girlie. You're just in the wrong place at the wrong time, boy."

I grab up the closest branch. It's not much, but it's the easiest thing I can snatch. I slam him in the back of his head as hard as I can. He swings around to face me. When he does, he loses his grip of Colt. I yelp as I see Colt fall feet first into the ravine.

Colt's gone. He's dead. I didn't help anything. Colt might

have overtaken him. I lost Colt. It's all my fault.

I'm so enraged, I can't see straight. This Merc will die even if I have to go with him. I sprint full throttle toward him. "I'm ready to die, you coward!" I squeal, and charge as fast as I can. I reach out to grab him, but he steps out of the way at the last minute and I stumble. I try to catch myself. I tumble headfirst. Not a good death is my last thought as I swan dive to a certain fatal end.

A jerking motion halts my forward thrust. I feel a death grip on my ankle. I smile as I see Colt hanging onto a vine with one hand and my ankle with another. He didn't go over. There's still a chance, but the vine won't hold us both for long. He's just extended the inevitable, but in a way that makes me happy. At least we'll go together and on our own terms.

A horrible scream pierces the silence. The Merc's flailing body sails over us and hits the bottom with a thud. How is that possible? Maybe we have a guardian angel looking out for us.

"Swing her up to me!" A voice yells out. "I'll get her. I'll pull you up after."

I dangle for a minute before I'm yanked up. I glimpse the arm of the uniform of the person who drags me to the dirt. It's a Merc! Are we going to be prisoners now? Worse, he'll turn us in for the bounty in trade for power or rewards. Either way our quest is over. Colt follows quickly using the vine to walk his way up the side, easy for him now without my added weight.

I turn to face the Merc—ready to pounce.

My heart leaps. I recognize him.

Chapter 4

I can't believe it. I swallow my breath. "Riley? How?"
Riley clutches me under my arms, drags me to my feet, and squeezes me in a long hug. "Is there ever a time when you aren't in trouble?"

Colt slaps him on the back. "Glad you happened by when you did or we wouldn't be here." He wallops him again so hard that Riley lunges forward and loses his grip on me.

I fight tears. "He's right. I'm so glad to see you. Once again you saved my life." I hug him again quick and let go. "What's going on with Mom and Gretel? Are they okay? But how..."

"Too many questions. In a minute." Riley slips his arms around both of our waists. "We need to get out of here right now."

"I'm not moving until I know that Mom and Gretel are okay."

"They are." He glances around with a suspicious look. "I'll tell you everything. I won't leave anything out. But it won't matter if we don't move because we won't be alive. Let's go, now!"

He's right. The sun threatens to give away our location. The forest is eerily silent, except for the painfully obvious exception of our gasping breaths and the snapping sounds of leaves as they are crushed under every step. Periodically, we stop and listen for enemy movement. Hearing none, we venture a little farther.

After winding our way down the path for a few minutes, Riley points to brush. "We need to get off the trail. I have no way of knowing if someone will be here, but I can tell you it will be a Merc one hundred percent of the time. Wish we had a good hiding place."

Colt's face lights up. "I know a place!" He glances at me. "Remember?"

We clomp through the underbrush. "The cave." I inhale in an excited breath. "We're going to our cave!"

Colt leads and I am relieved that he remembers where it is hidden. He signals our arrival to our secret place by motioning toward some bushes. He directs us to pull the overgrown greenery aside, revealing the shrub-covered door. We quickly enter.

"I've sneaked up here a few times hoping to find my Dad and the survivors from our rescue, but they didn't make it." He drops his shoulders. "This was the rendezvous point. I thought he would have at least left me a note to tell me where they ended up."

I knew Colt sneaked off the farm some, but I had not thought he was looking for his family. I am so focused on saving my own family that I forget others have family too.

He shoves the brush around. "No one else has been here. See? No sign anyone ever came to this cave."

A dejected look erases my grin. I pat his back and I follow him through the door.

Colt picks up matches conveniently propped up by the door, easily lights a kerosene lantern, and illuminates the contents of the haven. Boxes of jarred and canned foods, some half-opened, are scattered about. I see the discarded jars of fruits we consumed last time we were here. Colt's right, no one has visited since we left. Huge water jugs rest on the dirt floor. It still smells musty like the barn back on the farm after it's been closed up for the winter.

I pick up a jar and open it. I take in a big whiff savoring the sweet aroma. "Peaches, my favorite. Let's eat!""

We plop down in the middle of the cave surrounded by the food and the water jugs. The other two open jars too and for the next few moments, slurping sounds fill the air.

Colt swallows a piece of fruit whole. "Riley, about time you tell us what's going on."

"Let me start by saying that I'm glad you are both alive. For the longest time, I thought you had been carried off and executed. Wasn't that what was supposed to happen?" Riley tosses another piece of fruit in his mouth.

Colt picks up the jug of water. "Yeah. Our sentence was commuted to life imprisonment on the farm. That's where we've been since then. The guards actually took us there." He turns up the jug and starts gulping water.

"Save some for me." I try to pull the jug down. "Yeah, we weren't supposed to leave. We were on farm arrest. We were supposed to stay there forever."

Riley chuckles. "And of course you decided not to follow orders. Why does that not surprise me?"

I giggle. A little water dribbles on my shirt. "Riley, did you know that the Undesirables or Desirables as we now call them made it to the farm? They followed our buggy when we left."

"I heard that." Riley dabs my chin with his finger. "Missed a spot."

I push his hand away and wipe my mouth with the sleeve of my jacket. "What I want to know is why you're off the ship, and what happened to Mom and Gretel?"

Colt nods. "Yeah, what's going on with Gretel? Is she *really* okay?"

Riley slaps his stomach. "That's enough for me right now." He scoots to the side of the cave and leans back. "They're both fine. The ship is here for two weeks, and then it leaves for America. One of the guards let it slip last week that you two had been taken to the farm and let go."

I put the lid back on my jar of peaches. "It was a secret.

Do Mom and Gretel know?"

Riley shakes his head. "I thought it best not to tell them since I wasn't sure you were still alive. Sometimes the Mercs say something but in the end, it might not be true. I've seen them go back and kill the person." He drops his head. "The boy you just saw. Like him, he was supposed to be taken back to his parents."

I lean up. "Why didn't the Merc take him back to his parents? That was a child."

"Lazy." Riley shrugs and sighs.

"I don't understand." And I don't. What does being lazy have to do with being a cold-blooded killer? Riley is not making any sense.

"I was with the boy and the Merc." Riley shakes his head. "The Merc decided he didn't want to waste his time and energy taking the boy back to his parents. He thought it was easier to kill him. So he knocked the boy in the head at night and he was dead in the morning."

Colt jerks up from his leaning position. "Why couldn't you do anything? Couldn't you at least attempt to save the child?"

"I was sleeping when it happened." Riley slams back against the cave side. "What could I do?" Riley asks. "In the morning, the boy was dead. The Merc already had him tied to his horse to take to the ravine. He tried to tell me it was the right thing to do. It was easier to kill him and then report back we had taken the boy to his parents. He also said that we could say that the boy had an accident and died on the trail."

"That doesn't make sense. Why would someone do that?" I ask and look over at Colt. "Does that make sense to *you*?" Colt shakes his head

"Not at all. Of course, it doesn't make sense to good people." Riley twirls the half-empty jar of fruit on the dirt floor. "Unfortunately, we don't have many good people in the Mercs. Some are bloodthirsty criminals. The Merc organization gives them a legal outlet to murder."

"So sad." A tear runs down my face. "That child was supposed to be back with his parents and now he's dead and his parents will never know what happened to him."

Colt slides up against the cave wall and crosses his arms. "Why are you here, Riley? How did you find us?"

"I volunteered to go with the Merc to take the boy back. I was hoping to slip away and go by the farm and see if you two were still alive." Riley sighs. "When he killed that boy, I told him I was going to go back and report him, but he pulled a gun on me."

I shift on the floor. "He shot you?"

Riley taps the jar on the ground. "No, he shot *at* me. He didn't hit me, but he didn't know that. When the gun went off, it startled me so much that I lost my footing and fell down a hill. Fortunately, it was a short drop and just stunned me. Guess I was *still* long enough to convince him I was dead. I followed him when he left and..." He stops for a minute and shrugs. "You know the rest."

"We're glad you're here." Colt slaps Riley's leg. "Really glad or we'd be dead."

"We need to get Mom and Gretel off that ship." I rest my hands on my knees. "Will you help us?"

Riley stops moving. "Wait a minute." He furrows his brow. "I came here to find you and help you train for the resistance. I just escaped the ship. I don't want to go back." His shoulders droop. "I can't go back. They'll wonder what happened to the other Merc." He glares at me. "What about the people living on your farm? Are you just going to leave them?"

"Of course I'm going to find help for the people back at the farm. Colt and I are planning to search out other resistance groups. We heard they were all over. And then after that...I mean we have two weeks..." I let out an exasperated groan. "Don't you understand? If Mom and Gretel leave for America, I might not ever see them again. I *have* to get back on that ship."

"How?" Riley taps my forehead. "Everyone thinks you're dead."

I sit up against the cave wall and let out a deep breath. "That *is* a problem, but I'll figure out a way around it. I always do."

Colt nods. "That's true. What if we just concentrate on

trying to get Gretel and your mom *off* instead of us *on*?"

"That'll work." I cross my arms. "Now all we have to do is leave here." I hold my hand up, pointing one finger up, and count the rest as I list our tasks off. "Make sure we don't get caught by the Mercs, find other resistance groups, give them information about our farm, make sure that is working..." Running out of fingers on one hand, I start counting on the other. "Find our way to the ship, figure out a way to get Mom and Gretel off, make our way back to the farm with them, end human trafficking, defeat the royals and those not wanting democracy, and do all of that in..."

Colt laughs. " ... the next two weeks." He pauses. "We do have a bit more time for that end stuff."

"Exactly." Riley says, "No problem. Let's do all of that."

Riley catches my eye and starts laughing. I laugh too.

I know it's probably not appropriate, but I'm stressed. It's hard to live in fear for your life constantly. That laughing, that down to your toes, bottom of your stomach, fall on the floor laughing with my two best friends makes me feel better than I have felt in a long time. I need this and I'm sure that Colt and Riley do too.

It's been a hard few months. My world, and the entire world, has been turned upside down. The virus that kept us all separated is eradicated. Now it's all a battle for control, with the different sides lying, stealing, and manipulating—whatever it takes to make sure their side wins. It's a battle to choose the color of our future. I'm determined that in this new world, everyone will be free, democracy will win, and the royals will be nothing but figureheads with no real power.

Is that too much to ask?

Chapter 5

Our sense of urgency returns the next day. We refresh supplies and venture out with a new plan. First order of business, to find at least one of the small bands of resistance. Our farm children need some support. I wouldn't feel good about it, if we don't at least try to send them some help. If we get enough small groups together, we might become a force to be reckoned with. We might actually make a difference. What a nice positive thought! I try to hold onto that positivity all day long.

I refuse to think about Mom and Gretel too much. If I do, I'll run full force to Hamburg. That wouldn't be wise. I need to be smart so I am not caught. Only problem is that finding people who are trying very hard not to be found proves a difficult task.

We come across no one for two days, as we travel towards the ship. Occasionally, I notice the gorgeous countryside. I feel guilty enjoying its beauty. We need to complete our mission. The longer we go without seeing anyone, the more discouraged I become.

On the third day, we close in on Hamburg, the town

where the ship is docked. I hear a rustling in the forest. I crouch into the brush alongside the trail. "Colt!" I whisper, but he doesn't hear me.

A young girl about seven years old sprints down the trail and runs full throttle into Colt. She crashes into him and he grabs her arm.

She yells, "You can't take me. I won't tell you anything!" She kicks him hard, but he holds fast.

"I didn't ask you anything." Colt clutches the squirming girl. "Quit kicking!"

The girl freezes for a moment and shouts, "Are you a Merc?"

Colt shakes his head. "No." He rubs his chin. "Are you?"

"No! Girls can't be Mercs, everyone knows that!" The girl spies Riley. "Even if you're not, he is." She twists out of Colt's arms, lands hard on the ground, and falls backward into a prickly bush. "Ouch!"

I squat beside the girl. "Are you okay?" I grab her hand and pull her out of the bush. "Sit here on the trail for a minute."

She cuddles up to me and I pull the thorns out of her arm. "I know *you're* not a Merc." She says, "You're a girl. Did they catch you?"

"No. I'm Paisley." I nod toward the others. "These are my friends, Colt and Riley. Who are you, and why are you running?"

"Kelley, my name is Kelley." She wipes the dirt off her pants. "I'm running from Mercs. They're trying to capture me and make me work for them. Like a slave."

I sit beside her, pick up her foot, and retie her shoelaces. "Where are you supposed to be?"

"Not supposed to say."

"There." I pat her neatly tied shoe. "Why can't you say?"

"It's a secret. We cause problems. I find out where the Mercs are and I go back and report. But they saw me and started chasing me." She flexes her feet in front of her, admiring her laces. "I can't tie them that good. They always come untied." She smiles at me.

Riley says, "She could be part of a resistance group.

That's the people we've been looking for." Riley sits down beside Kelley. "Tell us where they're located."

"I'm not telling you anything, Merc," responds Kelley, jutting out her chin.

I rub her hair. "First, we all need to hide so the Mercs don't find us. Then we'll tell you who we are and what we're about. Okay? Will you come with us?"

She studies me for a few minutes. She frowns at Riley, and then looks at Colt. She half-smiles before refocusing on me. Her face breaks into a full grin. "I know a place where no one will find us. Come on."

"Lead the way." I stand up and pull her to her feet.

Colt squints his eyes. "Are you sure about this? It could be a trap!"

"Even if it is, do we really have a choice?" I whisper to him. "I hope she's taking us to the rest of her clan. Maybe we can convince the others in her group."

Colt smiles. "You're always thinking."

I feel the edges of my mouth curl. "I'm always doing that, but sometimes I *think* us right into trouble. Like right now, we really don't have time for this. We need to get to Hamburg and onto that ship."

"You're right. We *also* need to find some help for our people. Let's hope we can do both." Colt hugs me. "Remember, I want to get to that ship as bad as, or worse, than you do."

I sigh and nod. "I know. Gretel."

Colt waves his hand at the trail. "Lead on, Kelley."

For the next half-hour, we wander the German forest in a serpentine pattern, circling around and back more times than I can count. I'm not sure if she's doing it on purpose, but if someone put me at the starting point and asked me to retrace our steps, it would be impossible. A great tactic, one I had hoped to teach the charges back at our farm. Unfortunately, time ran out and plans sometimes have to be broken. Flexibility must be the rule if we plan to make any headway in the war. Hard to do when your family is so close yet so far and you ache to see them.

The green countryside is alive making it a little easier to maneuver. In a few weeks, winter will set in. Snow-covered trails make it harder to hide footprints unless the snow falls constantly.

Kelley runs ahead. I turn to Colt. "I have a bad feeling about this." We are standing in the middle of a clearing. Kelley is nowhere in sight.

"Don't move!" A loud voice bellows from the woods. In a few moments, five large boys surround us. "Identify yourself and give us the word." They hold huge sticks.

"We don't know the word." I say without thinking. Not a great idea since we might be clubbed to death any minute now.

"Stop, these are my friends." Kelley emerges from out of the forest leading a horse-pulled carriage. Its only inhabitant is an age-weathered woman with a shawl draped around her shoulders. "Make them stop, Aunt Sandra!"

Aunt Sandra is helped out of the carriage by a couple of the boys. She doesn't say anything. The boys still have their makeshift weapons held above their heads, but they stand still while the woman hobbles around, studying each of us. She stops at me. "You saved my niece?"

"Yes." I nod. "We all did." I motion to Riley and Colt.

One of the boys pipes in. "This one's a Merc, Auntie." He grabs Riley's bare arm, revealing his Merc tattoo. Riley jerks his arm away.

"Quiet, boy!" Aunt Sandra looks at me. Her eyes squint almost closed. "Do you want to tell me what's going on?"

Colt opens his mouth to speak and Auntie holds up a gnarled hand. "Not you, *her*." She points at me.

"It'll take a few minutes." I manage.

She shuffles into the forest a ways and pulls back the brush to reveal a circle of rocks. "We better have a seat then."

All five boys take seats on the single rocks. Auntie, Kelley, and I huddle together on the same long rock, leaving Colt and Riley to sit on the dirt. I tell them of our troubles. I'm not quite sure if I should reveal everything, but I do. I know I'm taking a chance, but our time to get to the ship is growing short. If we have any hope to reach Mom and Gretel in time, we have to trust someone. They listen intently, not interrupting, even when I explain how Riley became a part of us because he was an Uncounted who had been recruited by the Mercs. I tell them that he was born on a farm in the Bavarian forest not too far from where I live. So in reality, he wasn't really a Merc, but a farm person like me.

I stop when I finish my story. Aunt Sandra rubs her chin. "I think that joining the resistance groups together is a great idea. Since you plan to go to the ship, you'll have to trust my boys to go to your farm and help your little ones. Do you trust me?"

"Is this your family?" I ask.

"Yes." She looks at the boys with fondness and love.

I stare at her. "These children that I told you about may not be my blood, but they are my family. I need to know you are telling me the truth before I give you information about where to find them."

One of the boys asks, "Even if we threaten to kill you."

I nod. "I'd die before I put them in harm's way."

Aunt Sandra studies me for a moment then says, "I believe you just might do that." A boy helps Aunt Sandra limp to her feet. "We'll show you so you'll know you can trust us."

The same boy cocks his head. "You sure? They may be lying. This may be a trick to find our hiding place."

"I'm not lying. I promise." I bow slightly in her direction. A sign of respect.

"They aren't." Aunt Sandra hobbles to the carriage and gets back in. She pulls Kelley in beside her and says, "Follow us."

"I'm grateful to you," I say.

Aunt Sandra motions to the other boys to get Riley and Colt to their feet. "I've lived a long time. I've seen a lot. I know when I'm being fed a story. In a few minutes, you'll see we aren't lying to you either."

Our group tramps deep into the forest until we come upon a vineyard with vines so thick they are almost impassable. We make slow progress until we come to a clearing. In front of us stands a large concrete barrier fence covered with greenery. Until you are standing right in front of it, it is completely hidden.

"Does this wall go all the way around?" I ask.

"Yeah," A boy who hasn't talked before answers.

One of the boys finds a tree and starts counting a path around the wall. He counts his steps to one hundred and thirty four before he stops. He reaches into the mass of vines and locates a gate. It takes him a few minutes to unlock the latches. Aunt Sandra gets out of the carriage and the boys hide the coach in a hollow area in the bushes and cover it with brush.

I'm surprised when we walk into darkness instead of light. "Is this a cave?"

"Yes." The same boy answers. "Duck or you'll bump your head." When we all clear the gate and crouch in the cave, he turns the handle on the latch. "It's a secret, how you open it from the inside. Just in case someone breaks in, we can trap him or her here. My brothers and I built this cave. You like it?"

I nod. He doesn't respond. It's dark so I guess he can't see my gestures. I mumble, "Yeah." In a few feet, we are able to stand without crouching.

One of the other boys retrieves a lamp and lights it. We walk a good distance before we come upon two sentries guarding a threshold. They bow when they spy Aunt Sandra. We are allowed to pass. A few more steps lead to another door that opens into an unbelievable sight.

A high hedge blocks our passage. About a kilometer ahead beyond the maze sits a sprawling tall structure, its pinnacle castle-like in its appearance. From this vantage point, we can see it is crowned by several tower spikes.

The boys take a piece of cloth and blindfold the three of us.

Riley holds the cloth over his eyes while someone ties it behind his head. "You *are* serious about no one finding you."

I cringe a little as they tie the cloth over my eyes. "I'm not a fan of blindfolds." I flash back to being blindfolded and supposedly being led to my death that turned out to be house arrest, but just the same, it isn't a happy thought.

Colt quietly lets them blindfold him. He whispers to the

group. "Anything that will get me a step closer to saving Gretel, I'm okay with."

Aunt Sandra says, "The boys will take each of you by the arm and lead you through the maze." It takes a little while and we bump into the sides and stumble on the uneven terrain. A couple of turns we go forward then backwards, one time we have to jump over what sounds like a stream. We have to climb a ladder to move ahead at one point. Blindfolded or not, if you didn't know how to get through this maze or have a map, I don't think you'd make it. It must be quite a puzzle, and huge as it takes a while.

Finally, our blindfolds are removed. In front of us stands the most magnificent castle I've ever seen. The structure sits in a valley like a crown cushioned on a pillow. Its regal splendor begs for a royal bow of respect. It's surrounded by forested hills on all sides and is hidden mostly by the natural terrain. Spires of stone with triangular spiked crests and a gazillion gated walls mesh together in an intricate pattern that rivals what I read about Versailles. I don't know how they ever kept this a secret.

A deep valley devoid of water surrounds the structure. We follow Aunt Sandra across an open drawbridge. The inside structure houses a mammoth courtyard where giggly children run, holding waving flags. Kelley says a quick good-bye as she joins the fun with the rest of the children. A metalwork shop and stables for horses are located near the entrance.

What kind of place is this? I squint and make out a structure even farther up the mountainous hill. It looks like the pictures of ruins where wealthy landowners would build gigantic castles at the highest point of their land to not only watch and rule over their kingdom, but as a vantage point to ward off enemy attacks. Men roam the ruins and I wonder if they are operating the same type outlook post now.

Colt, Riley, and I shoot glances at each other as we make our way to the main structure. The two men guarding the gate bow slightly to Aunt Sandra and open the massive outside doors that allow us to pass into the main house. Colorful rugs of all shapes and sizes lay on the floor. People sit around on the rugs. Some are sewing. Some read aloud or to themselves. Some are talking.

When Aunt Sandra enters, the room immediately falls silent. They all stand and bow. She makes her way to the center and sits on a simple chair of wood and iron, devoid of any decoration. The chair is surrounded by more rugs. She indicates that we all sit.

"This is my house," Aunt Sandra says. "My family owns these lands, and I have been sheltered by this house my whole life."

I shift my legs out in front of me. "Even during the virus outbreak and quarantine?"

"Especially then. One of my son's friends worked on the military base and we got word immediately what was happening. Some of his friends were mistakenly left during the evacuation. My son brought his friends and some of the villagers here. From time to time, we have brought others into our hidden sanctuary. We are self-sufficient. We grow our own food. We have been undetected for all these years."

"You're showing me this so I'll trust you, right?" I ask.

She smiles. "Of course, dear. I want to help your... what did you call them...Undesirables."

"They're Desirables now."

"Of course they are, my dear. Everyone here is desirable too. Please let me help you."

I look over at Riley and Colt. "What do you think?" They both nod. Why would she show us this if she wasn't planning to help us?

I tell her about the farm and its location. I explain who is there and what shape they are in physically, being specific about their disabilities, injuries, and limitations. She shares some information she has garnered from the outside. It's dire. The king is gaining support for a dictatorship of the world with him as its master and chief.

"That can't happen," I tell her. "He is a bad king!"

She nods. "I know." She sighs. "The information my couriers have brought back paint a picture of children being kidnapped to be used to serve the rich. Horrible stories of mistreatment. It must be stopped."

I glance at some flyers on her table. An advertisement for the Sponsored Companion Doll Program catches my eye, and I point to it. "We were Sponsored Companions, living dolls for the princess." I stop for a moment, frowning at the glossy advertisement. "Anyone who they don't deem as in perfect health, they label as undesirable. Anyone without a family, they label as Uncounted. I was an Uncounted."

"Then you have firsthand knowledge of how it is. I have one more thing to show you." She hobbles toward one side of the room. We follow her through the doors. Inside are beds filled with people with varying degrees of injuries.

"What's this?" I point to a bottle hanging upside down.

"This is our hospital." She hugs a woman carrying a clipboard. "We conduct raids on the Mercs. We confiscate medical supplies, radios, weapons, food, all sorts of things. We smuggle them back here to supply our army. We plan to take back Europe. At first, we had to wait to make sure that the virus was truly eradicated. We've just been waiting for the right time."

Colt picks up a pill bottle. "Some of ours could use some medical care." He picks up a yellowed newspaper. "Do you get news from the outside?"

Aunt Sandra smiles at a patient sleeping in a bed. "Some. We have actually used their news sources to find out where and when shipments are coming. You wouldn't believe the medicines we found."

Riley, silent for a while, pipes up. "Some people are trying to organize the Consortium of the World."

Aunt Sandra fluffs a patient's pillow as she talks to us. "I've heard that. What are your thoughts on that matter?"

I offer, "We used to work for the ambassador. I think he's trying to bring democracy back."

"I've heard he was a good man, but the king..." She shakes her head.

Colt huffs. "Don't get us started. The king is not one of our favorite people. It might have to do with the fact that he sentenced me and Paisley to death."

"You're not dead." Aunt Sandra pinched her lips together. "Why is that?"

"Too long of a story. But he's right, the king did try to have us killed. But the ambassador is really nice, an honest man. He would be good to lead our world into a democratic rule."

"Come, come." She walks towards the door. "We must let these nurses and doctors get back to work." As she reaches the door, she turns. "What are your plans now?"

"If you promise to take care of the people at my farm, we'll continue from here to try to rescue my family."

"I give you my word. I ask only that if you come across any others in trouble or on the same quest as us that you send them our way. If you're not sure if they're telling you the truth, don't worry about it. It'll be fine. My boys and I will figure out if they're truthful or not." She bows slightly. "You are welcome back here when you find your family."

"Are you joking?" Riley laughs. "We would never be able to find this place again."

"You don't have to. My boys will find you. They always do." She motions to a huge table heaped with fresh fruits and other foods. "But first, eat. Stay the night and start fresh in the morning."

"Sounds like a plan." I take a seat and chomp into the best-looking pear I've seen in a long time.

I feel safe. Even if it's only for a night.

Chapter 6

We venture out on our new mission after being awakened. Better than an alarm clock, children run around the compound signaling the start of the day. "Time to wake up! Time to wake up!" they yell until everyone is awake. Makes me wonder who wakes *them* up.

Fortunately, Aunt Sandra sends a guide to help us off their land and point us in the direction of Hamburg. It takes a while to get back through the maze, through the entrance cave, and out of the surrounding woods. We would have never found it.

We estimate it will take us three full days to reach the port town. With our food rationed and our path clear, the only obstacle standing in our way is the ever-present danger of being discovered. Mercs roam the countryside with no formation or clear plan, making them impossible to guard against.

Two and a half days in, while searching for a place to rest, we find a group of children huddled in a cave. After sharing the few morsels of food we have, we tell them about Aunt Sandra. We give them specific directions to find the area close to the sanctuary.

I say, "Don't worry. When you get close, they'll find you. Take care." We send them on their way with a message to Aunt Sandra, that we have almost made it to Hamburg.

A large hill stands in front of us.

"We're almost there." I breathe. "I can smell the ocean."

Riley points to a seagull circling in the sky. "You're right."

We scale the hill and crawl on our bellies to peer over the side. The color of the terrain has changed somewhat from the lush green to bald bushes, announcing the change of season. Fall has always been my favorite time of year. I loved the weather and the anticipation of snow. Always loved the winter too. It meant no chance of Mercs. Now winter means it's too hard to travel. Strange how situations change your outlook.

"There it is." Riley points out the obvious. The stack protrudes from above the deck of the great ship. "I don't know how we're going to get on it."

I flip from my belly to my back. "We'll figure out a way."

"You always do." Colt stands and pulls me up. "No one down there to see us. If we're going to get Gretel, we have to stand tall and make it happen."

Riley flips over to his back and grabs at my leg. "We're taking a chance. You are both on house arrest. If I'm caught, I'll be thrown in the brig for abandoning my post."

"Take a chance, Riley. Stand up. They probably think you're dead anyway." I pull at him.

Riley stands up beside us. "We need to be careful, whatever we do."

"I've got a crazy idea." I hoist on my backpack.

"Why does that not surprise me?" Colt chuckles. "Give it to us."

"Let's go back to the doll store and try to get sold to the royals as Sponsored Companions again." I take off running down the hill.

Riley yells after me. "That *is* a crazy idea." He pauses for a minute. "Or stupid."

Colt catches up to me. "I agree with Riley. Stupid. You

want us to be owned as dolls to play with the children of the rich again. That doesn't make sense." Riley runs alongside and Colt continues, "They would recognize us. Plus didn't we get tattoos?"

I shout to him as I run. "Tattoos! That's right! My temporary is worn off." We all stop to catch our breath halfway down. "Let's at least go by the store," I plead. "To see if it's a possibility. There are more rich people on that ship, besides the royals. We could be owned by someone else and probably stay out of their way."

Colt nods. "It's such a crazy idea that it just might work. To the doll store." He takes off after me as I run again.

Riley follows us and says, "Only if *I* get to play with the princess this time."

Entering the town of Hamburg is easier this time around. We don't smell as bad as we did the first time. We don't draw much attention as we navigate the streets looking for the doll store. The alley is easily recognizable because of its proximity to the ship and the shouts of the street vendors. Locating the alley gives us a starting point, which makes it easier to find the doll store. Peering in the window, we see Ms. DeVane sitting, prim and proper, while tending to a patron. It's been a while. Will she recognize us?

"Let's sneak in the back like before and see if they have any new costumes. We might be able to pull it off if we just put on a new outfit." Colt flattens against the alley wall adjacent to the store.

"I'm with you." Riley settles in beside Colt. "Remember, I haven't been here before."

"We look like we're criminals with you two pressed against the alley wall like we're under arrest or hiding or something. C'mon you two." I walk nonchalantly toward the store picking up brochures from the kiosks that sit in front of its door. "Wait until she isn't looking," I whisper to Colt.

It doesn't take long. Ms. DeVane turns her back to show a customer a doll.

Colt leads the way, crouching along the back aisle,

through the doors, and into the back storeroom. "Here we are once again. In the doll birthing room."

Riley scrunches his face. "Birthing room?"

I pick up a doll from the trash bin. "He's just joking. Don't listen to him. It looks just the same as it did before."

Riley thumbs through a pamphlet. "More propaganda for the king. Rubbish!"

Colt proudly displays a poster. "New Dutch Dolls," he reads off. The poster displays a picture of two people dressed in the traditional dress of Holland. The female wears a white triangular hat crossway on her head, a blue-checkered dress, with a white apron and wooden shoes. The boy is dressed in navy knee-length pants, a navy blazer, a white shirt, a blue cap, and wooden shoes.

I look around and spy a box labeled: *New/Just In*. I open it. Wrapped inside the box is a pair of complete costumes, one for a boy and one for a girl, representing Holland. "These are brand new. The people from the boat can't possibly have them yet. This just might work."

Riley sighs and picks up the outfit. "It will for you two, but not for me. What are we going to do with two boys, one girl, and only one of each outfit?" He sits on the floor, head in hands. "I really want to help, but I can't chance getting caught. I wouldn't even be able to lie my way out of this. I've been gone way too long. Lamar will know, if he's still there."

"Lamar? I hope he's not still there. I can't stand that guy." I slump down beside Riley. "If he is, we'll figure out something." That Merc, Lamar, is one of the most bloodthirsty Mercs I've come across. He wants to kill all the time. Most of the time his conquests are the Undesirables, people with disabilities, or those weaker than him. He probably preys on them because they will be less likely to be missed. It's so sad! I had a dream once that Lamar got his due. His arm was burned badly and he became an Undesirable. That would make him think twice about wanting to kill people who aren't perfect physically.

Colt hasn't moved. He stands by the boxes looking at the outfits and studying the wooden shoes. "I have a much better idea." He brings the shoes over and sits down beside us. "What if you and Riley went as the dolls?" He points to the shoes. "Believe me, I don't want to wear this get up, especially not these."

I frown. "Are you going to just stay here on shore?" I slap Colt hard on the arm. "That's not very nice. What about Gretel? I thought you couldn't live without her. That's all you've been moaning about since we got to the farm."

Colt grabs my hands and holds them down. "Hear me out. What if you two went as the dolls and I take Riley's clothes and go in as a Merc?"

I jump up, hands on my hips. "A Merc? Are you out of your mind? What do you know about being a Merc?" I look over at Riley. "Tell him, Riley, tell him why that won't work. Tell him why that's the craziest idea you've ever heard. Tell him, Riley."

Riley sits, silent.

I flop back down. "You're not thinking this is a *good* idea are you? How can he pass?"

"The only real thing he needs that he doesn't have is a Merc tattoo. The only thing I would need to do would be to hide my Merc tattoo and get a Holland doll tattoo." Riley pulls up his sleeve.

"It can't be done then." I shake my finger at Riley. "Do you know how to hide a tattoo, or make one?" I wag my finger at Colt. "Do you?"

Colt and Riley both lean out and look at each other.

"Any ideas?" Riley asks.

"One." Colt gets up and walks toward the door to the store. "But it's a gamble."

The two of us follow Colt into the store. Ms. DeVane sits quietly focused on a piece of paper. There are no customers.

Colt approaches the counter and gently rubs his fingers on the wood to get her attention, and he meekly talks. "Ms. DeVane I don't know if you remember us but I'm about to bet my life that you are not going to turn us in, and that you will, in fact, help us."

Riley and I freeze, fearful of the answer we are about to

get. What if Ms. DeVane turns us in? Then all of this has been for nothing. We travelled for nothing. We might even be tortured into giving up the location of our farm or Aunt Sandra's compound. How long would I be able to hold out? I don't know. Torture, I don't know how much I could take without folding. I don't want to find out. All of these horrible thoughts run through my head for what seems like forever.

Ms. DeVane sits and quietly studies us. She reaches under her desk. She's probably going to bring out a gun to shoot us dead or take off into the street to announce our presence. What kind of trouble has Colt gotten us into?

Chapter 7

Ms. DeVane moves in slow motion. I hold my breath wondering what will come out from under that desk. She pulls out a piece of paper and slaps it on the table. I gasp!

"Are you okay?" Ms. DeVane peers out at me from under her starkly cut bangs.

"Uh-huh?" I manage to answer weakly before my body relaxes.

Colt fingers the end of the paper, trying to pull it across the desk to him. "What's this?"

Snatching it back, Ms. DeVane lifts her sleeve exposing the back of her upper arm and reveals an etched tattoo of a broken egg. "I'm with the resistance. Thought you might need some assurances." She quickly rolls the sleeve back down. "Of course that part of me must stay hidden. You understand, don't you?"

I nod in disbelief.

Colt's mouth drops open and he asks, "How long?"

The corners of her mouth turn into a shy smile. "Like I thought you were *really* Sponsored Companions." She shrugs. "I figured if the royals didn't know any better... and if you two had enough of a reason to get on the ship that you were willing to lie to get on illegally." She chuckles. "Let's just say, I thought it was my duty to help you." She shuffles the paper. "This is just for show in case someone comes in. You are asking me about buying a doll." She peers over at me. "And by you, I mean *you*, not the boys." She picks up a pen. "Now what can I help you with?"

I sit in the chair in front of the desk. "It's complicated."

She taps the desk with her pen. "I'm okay with that."

Riley pulls up his military jacket sleeve to reveal *his* Merc "M." "It's a little more complicated than you might have thought."

Ms. DeVane motions to the empty seats in front of her desk. "You two have a seat."

Colt and Riley flop into the chairs. A patron, sporting an elaborate hat full of pink feathers surrounding a white glittered bird, saunters in, carrying a blonde dog with a pink ribbon tying up a tuft of hair.

"Be with you in just a minute." Ms. DeVane pushes a page over in front of us. "If you'll look over this contract while I help this customer. I'll be back with you in a minute." She fires us a quick look and disappears down one of the aisles.

Riley shifts around to look for others. Seeing none, he turns back to us and whispers, "I say we just lay the plan out. Tell her exactly what we need and see what she can do."

I nod. He's right. No use trying to candy coat it or manipulate her. If we hope to get on that ship, we need Ms. DeVane's help.

The bell sounds at the front of the store indicating an arrival or departure of a customer. We are hoping for the latter. Our wish is granted. Ms. DeVane takes her seat behind the desk in a couple of seconds. "What do you need?"

The three of us explain our plan. We tell her of my family on the ship and a little of our journey since we last saw her, omitting the gorier events like the killing of the boy and the biggest secret, the existence of Aunt Sandra's sanctuary. Ms. DeVane listens intently, writing notes on her paper as we talk.

"The Holland dolls, I can do." She opens her file and

pulls out a folder. "In fact, there is a couple on the ship who have an order in for the Holland Living Dolls for their seven year old. I can easily fake the papers and the tattoos." She reaches for Riley. "Let me see your Merc tattoo." She pulls his arm over and studies it for a moment. "Yes, it can be done. Plus with this as a guide I can put a temporary on for Colt." She leans back in her chair. "I can do all of this for you, but I want something in return."

I slump back in my chair and sigh.

Ut-oh here it comes.

Chapter 8

What can Ms. DeVane possibly want in exchange? She is going to fake papers and copy tattoos. That's worth a lot. What if the favor is too big? We all scoot closer to her desk waiting for our hopes to be squashed.

"I have a son. He was taken as an Uncounted three years ago. I want you to see if you can find out where he is. Come back here and tell me after you get your family off the ship." She lifts her eyeglasses to wipe a stray tear.

I squeeze her hand. "What's his name?"

"William," she whispers meekly. "He has blonde hair and the cutest smile." She stops and sighs. "He used to have the cutest smile. He also has a scar above his eye from when he fell off his bike. And a birthmark on his leg. It's in the shape of..." She buries her head in her hands.

I stand up, walk around her desk, and hug her. "How old is William?"

"Eight." She glances up to the ceiling for a minute. "He was five when they took him."

Colt says, "Do you know who took him or where?"

"The Mercs, of course. But where?" She shakes her head. "Not sure. I heard rumor to America, but I don't know for sure."

I look at the others and walk back around the desk to face her. "I'm going to be honest with you. We can promise to do everything we can to find information about your William, but in the end we might not be able to tell you anything." I clasped her hands in both of mine. "I don't want to promise you something that I'm not sure we can deliver."

Riley leans in. "It's hard to find the missing. They send them as far away from home as they can to keep them from escaping. Look what happened with me."

"If you want to back out on our agreement, since we can't promise you results, we totally understand," Colt says. "It wouldn't be right for you to take all of these risks."

Ms. DeVane scribbles on the paper. "Of course I'm going to help you. If it's possible, I want you to look for him or information. I might not ever know where my sweet William ended up, but I have to try to find out." She stares at us with a tear-streaked face. "You understand, don't you?"

I sit and clutch her hand. "Of course, we will do what we can."

Riley pokes at the paper. "Give us his full name. Date of birth. Any other identifiers like that birthmark or something unusual about him. We will see what we can do. Absolutely! Who knows? We might just get lucky and bring him back."

She smiles. "Wouldn't that be wonderful?" She motions to the back of the store. "You two..." She points at Riley and me. "Go get dressed in the traditional Holland outfit. It's in the back in a..."

Riley finishes her sentence. "A box. Yeah we already opened it. Sorry."

Riley and I go to change into our new garb. When we return, Colt's arm is elevated, protecting his newly drawn Merc tattoo. "See?"

"Unbelievable! It looks like the real thing!" I smile at Ms. DeVane. "Great job! You *are* an artist!" I pull my white apron out and curtsy. "What do you think of me as a little Dutch girl?" I ask Colt.

"Cute! Cute!" He thumbs-up with his free hand. "Where's Riley?"

Riley sheepishly ambles out of the dressing room. "Now I see what you mean, Colt. I feel like an idiot in this."

I nod. "But it's for Gretel and Mom."

Riley points to Ms. DeVane. "And William."

Ms. DeVane works quickly drawing the SC tattoos on Riley and me. We leave her store with hugs, information about William, and legal boarding papers.

"Feels like we've done this before." Colt pulls out the postcard from the kiosk as we pass by with the picture of the Neuschwanstein Castle. "Where Dreams Come True," remember?"

It was sweet of Colt to remember the postcard from my mother's treasure box. I tell Riley about a postcard from Orlando with the same picture of a castle from America that had that saying. I smile as I tell the story, but it only makes me more homesick to see my mother. I hate that she thinks I am dead. How horrible for her.

I smile and rub my fingers over the postcard before placing it back in its holder. "Do you think we'll be able to see the princess or the ambassador?" I can't tell either of them that I not only hope to rescue my mother and sister, but I really want to see the ambassador.

Riley crinkles his brow. "What reason would you have for wanting to see any of the royals?"

"The ambassador *did* save us." Colt spouts the truth although he doesn't know the entire story. The ambassador told me before I was forced off the ship that he was my real father. It's tough to get news like that and not be able to talk to him about it. Thankfully, I did get to have a conversation with my mother who confirmed his story. She found me wandering alone after the virus outbreak, took me in, and raised me as her own, a fact that made me love her even more.

"We *really* need to get on that ship." I quicken my walk.

Colt takes one step to my every two. "I agree. I *have* to see Gretel."

As we walk, Riley coaches Colt about how to act like a Merc. We decide that Colt will take us in with our papers. Our hope is that no one will inspect Colt or his tattoo too closely. We label that Plan A, then we discuss Plan B, running. Finally, we discuss Plan C, which is how to escape if we are caught. I shake my head at the boys. "I guess our real plan is that plan A or B better work."

We share an uncomfortable laugh as we spot the gangplank to the ship. The former name— "Queen Mary IV"— rests as a shadow under the new moniker in bolder brighter lettering, "Queen Nalani," the name of the king's daughter, the ambassador's wife, and the princess's mother. The ship is massive with at least fifteen floors. Colt and I spent a month traveling up and down them.

The ship has been docked for a week now, so the hustle and bustle is minimal. I don't know if that is a good or bad thing. We hang back to watch for movement. The timing is critical. One wrong move and it's Plan C whether we like it or not.

A huge group of patrons following a guide cuts in front of us. The tour guide bellows, "Stay with our group. You are very fortunate to have been granted permission to tour this great ship, *The "Queen Nalani."* This ship leaves for America in three days. King Ahomana asks that you consider this a small payment for your support in the upcoming election. Search your hearts! Is it really better for the people to have a democracy? We can have a democracy any time, but King Ahomana should be making those choices for us. He will know the best plan of action. He is a brilliant king."

I shake my head and mouth, "Really" to Riley and Colt. I can't believe my ears. This is the king who wanted Colt and I executed. This is the king trying to kill the ambassador, his own son-in-law. The king and the Mercs want to have complete and total power over the world. Don't they see? Don't they know? How can anybody possibly believe these lies? But here they are seventy or so men and women, listening intently to this speech, savoring every word, as if it was the rarest chocolate they would ever have. No, worse than that, listening to his jargon as if it were completely true.

The man continues talking, "Thank you. The king appreciates your support. After our tour is completed he asks that any or all of you feel free to join him for a king's banquet in the great dining hall." He motions to the group. "Follow me."

"This is our chance." I scrunch behind the large collection of people being funneled to the thin gangplank. Riley and Colt follow suit and we all finagle our way to the middle of the crowd. I tell them we'll worry about security later if we need to.

A redheaded woman dressed in a blue blazer pushes up to me. "I can't believe they are crowding us in like this. Don't they know who we are?"

I nod, not wanting to say anything for fear of giving our deception away. She continues, "I love that Amsterdam sent you in the native dress. What a nice touch! Do you speak the Hollands?"

I don't have to answer, thank goodness, as she is pushed back behind me and I lose sight of her. Although I can speak the Hollands, a Dutch language mix between German and English, my dialect might not be what she is expecting. I move farther up in the front of the mob. No one else attempts a conversation. I glance at Colt and Riley moving on through. They seem to be more interested in getting out of the close quarters than talking.

My instincts are right. It's too large of a crowd. Security is more worried about upsetting the king than they are about making sure that everyone in the group belongs. We walk with the others as they herd us into the first floor. We use them as cover for the three of us to escape down the stairs. We take two stairs at a time until we reach the tenth floor. No time to notice the disrepair this time, or the differences between the upper and lower floors. I remember how the floors are so luxurious on the top and dwindle as we descend to the tenth floor. A floor we know well since it is where all of the Sponsored Companions are housed. It's the floor we spent most of our time on when we were on the ship before.

Colt says, "Let's stop here. We have three days before we sail."

I scrunch my face and look at him. "How do you know that?"

He smiles. "It was the only part of the speech I listened to."

"Let's see if we find any of the SCs." Riley pushes us down the corridor.

We round the corner. I come face to face with Suma, the female Sponsored Companion doll from Egypt. "Suma," I whisper.

Her eyes get wide. She faints.

Colt catches her. "So much for subtle entrances."

Chapter 9

"Good thing I remember how to open the door." Colt carries Suma down the hall. "Which is hers?"

I smile and point. "Good thing I remember which room is hers."

Riley pushes us forward. "Quit patting yourselves on the back. We need to get out of the hallway."

Colt waves Suma's wrist in front of the door lock. It opens. Naeem, her brother, stands as we invade his room. Riley covers his mouth before he has a chance to scream. "Remember Colt and Paisley?" He whispers.

Colt gently pats the back of Suma's hand as he delicately lays her on the bed. "Suma, Suma."

Suma wakes up with fear in her eyes for a quick moment before they fill with tears and she throws her arms around Colt's neck. She then reaches out for her brother and me. It's a few minutes before Suma releases any of us from her hug. I'm crying by this time.

Naeem plops on the edge of his bed and drops his head in his hands. "They told us you were dead. Said they killed you as an example for all of us."

I scoot in beside him. "Do we look dead?"

"No." He shakes his head. "I'm glad you're not, but why would they lie? What happened?"

Colt says, "They took us back to Paisley's farm and said we were to stay there for the rest of our lives, but the Undesirables tracked our horse and buggy. They've been with us ever since."

"We are still training for the war," I add. "We don't have many of the original adults. They're dying because they're sick and we don't have any medicines they need."

Suma sighs, "How sad. Who is taking care of them now that you're here?"

"We found some pockets of people who were with the resistance." Colt sits on the floor. "A couple headed back to the farm to help the children with their training."

Suma nods. "I'm so glad the children are alive. It worried me when they forced them to leave the ship."

"Do you ever see my Mom and Gretel?" I hate to be blunt, but Colt, Riley, and I need to find them and get off. We have three days to find them and plan our escape. Three days should give us time. Should be easy.

"They're still working in the same place. They're fine the times I've seen them. But they seem sad. Probably missing you, Paisley." She claps her hands. "We should go right now and surprise them, let them see you're alive!"

Riley overhears. "Be patient. I know you and Colt are anxious, but we have some time. Night might be a better cover. Let's wait."

Colt's shoulders droop. "Guess a few more hours won't hurt. We don't want to be caught."

I sigh, sharing his disappointment. "I'll try to wait, but it's going to be hard. I miss my family." I ask, "How's the princess?"

"Spoiled as ever." Suma laughs. "Miss Brita is still having a lot of trouble. She comes down in a wheelchair for the princess's lessons."

"Scoot." Riley pushes Colt over. "I want to sit too. What about the obstacle course and Lamar?"

Naeem lets out a long sigh. "The obstacle course was stopped because of Lamar. I heard the other day that he thought two of his Mercs had been killed. I think your name was one on the lists, Riley."

"Yes, that makes sense. I'm sure they thought we were killed on the trail." Riley crosses his arms. "Of course I am sure that Lamar's crying over the loss."

Naeem chuckles. "Not so much."

"The queen is bed-ridden." Suma leans around to talk directly to me. "She's having a difficult time with her pregnancy." She sits back. "The ambassador is worried about her, which is why we are heading back to America. There is supposed to be a doctor there who might be able to help her."

Colt stretches his legs out as much as he can. "A lot has changed."

Riley starts. "Then we found a castle where…"

I interrupt him. "Along the way we saw all kinds of castle ruins."

Riley shoots a confused frown my way. No time to explain to him now. We shouldn't share everything with these two. Some of these secrets could get them killed. I'm not sure if I'm telling myself that because I truly believe it or because the major betrayer last time was one of us SCs.

I have to ask, "How is Baako?"

The room goes silent for a minute. Suma is the first to speak. "He's been on the outside looking in. I think he thought when he turned us all in, he would get special treatment, but he hasn't. Lamar is still in charge and on a major power trip, killing for no reason. Scary times. We wonder if we can actually survive the travel to America." She averts her eyes. "Sometimes we talk among ourselves that you two were the lucky ones. At least you were out of this."

"But that would mean we were dead, Suma." Colt laughs. "I think it's better that we are alive."

"That's true." Suma continues, "Adanna, Baako's sister, was saved because of him and cries all the time. I feel so sorry for her."

Naeem pulls at my triangular white hat. "Why are you

dressed like this?" He waves his hand over at Riley. "Better yet, why is he dressed like a Sponsored Companion doll? Aren't you a Merc?"

Colt pulls up his sleeve. "I'm the Merc now."

Colt, Riley, and I spend the next few minutes explaining our plan to rescue my mom and sister, and then go back underground.

"You can't leave us here!" Suma buries her face in the bed cover and starts bawling. "You must stay and help us."

I shake my head. "Help you what?" I rub her hair. "I need to get my family off before they go to America and we can't find them."

Naeem folds his hands in front of his lap. "She wants you to stay to save the ambassador."

"The ambassador is still in danger?" I ask. "I thought he was heading back to America. Isn't he from there?"

"Miss Brita says they are holding his son hostage." Suma speaks through sobs. "They're going to kill his son in America if he doesn't do what the king says. It's so sad."

Naeem comforts his sister. "He has been so sad ever since you two left."

I know that I need to find my Mom and Gretel and save them. But I have to ask myself—can I really leave when my father is in danger if there is something I can do?

"We might be able to stay and help. Could we go to America?" I say before thinking.

Colt and Riley jump up at the same time. Colt towers over me. "What are you talking about?" He looks over to Naeem and Suma. "I mean, we would like to help, but you don't understand. Paisley and I are supposed to be at the farm, and Riley is a wanted Merc. We'll die if we stay. How would that help you?"

I need to be smart about how I phrase this. I can't force Colt or Riley to stay. In fact, if Colt and Riley would take Mom and Gretel back to the farm, then I could just stay and try to help my dad and save my brother. Even saying that inside my mind sounds crazy. What could I accomplish all by myself? Who could I trust to help me? The better question is who could

I possibly help? Could I save my brother all by myself? Was it possible? Probably not. I sigh loudly, ready to give up.

"I'll stay with you." Riley hugs me. "I owe you that much."

I look at Riley, such a good person. He doesn't owe me anything, but him saying he'll stay with me makes my stomach flip. I take a deep breath and manage to muster a question. "Where would we stay?"

"With us of course!" Suma stands and hugs me. "You and I can sleep on the bed together, and Naeem can take his bed and Riley can have the floor." She grins. "See, it's settled. We have it all figured out."

Colt pulls my arm. "Except the part where we save Gretel and your mom."

I hug up to him. "I thought we'd help you get them off the ship, and then you could take them back to the farm. When Riley and I get back, we'll find you."

A knock at the door interrupts the conversation. Riley, Colt, and I cram into the small bathroom while Naeem opens the door. A mumbled conversation goes on for a few minutes. Then all is quiet.

Naeem carefully opens the door and the three of us roll out. "That was news from the captain. You need to make your move in the next two hours. That's when we leave for America."

I tap my foot trying to come up with a plan. We all start a plan with "What if..." but we do not complete our thought. I guess we are all having the same trouble. What can you really do with only two hours left?

"We can't possibly get out of here. It would take us that long to find them. We're stuck." Colt decides for us. "It'll be cramped, but I guess I'll sleep in the tub." Colt places his cheek on top of my head. "You get your wish. We're *all* off to America, where all your dreams come true."

Chapter 10

The ship's speaker booms, "Decks one through ten are invited to the top deck to wave your good-byes as we move the ship from the port out into open ocean for our transatlantic cruise."

I squeeze around Riley who is standing in the middle of the floor, or what little there is of it, in the small cabin. "I need you all to get out of the way. I need to go to the bathroom for a minute. It can't wait."

Sitting on the toilet, I hear them discuss how we can't go to the top. "You might be recognized. This is going to be a tricky ride, not much room in here—" Naeem says, "—very close quarters and a long trip."

I remember seeing the map of the world before, the world is big. We're going to be on this ship an uncomfortably long time. I open the door of the water closet and announce, "We need to try to find Mom and Gretel and at least let them know we're alive. I wouldn't want to have either of them bump into us not knowing. How horrible would it be for them? Plus, they would most likely blow our cover with their reaction. They need to know as soon as possible. Could one of you tell them?" I look at Naeem.

Naeem squirms his way to the door and motions for Suma. "We can try. Right now, we will go to the top deck. At least there is more room there."

"I'm not sure this is going to work." Colt pulls up his sleeve and looks at his Merc tattoo. "It has Riley's identifiers and besides it's not real. I guess since I'm already on the ship and as long as I don't get off, there should be no security checks for my tattoo. Or at least, I hope not."

Riley nods. "I've never been checked on the ship so you're probably fine."

Colt bops me on the forehead. "That means that I can walk around and scout out another safe place to stay."

Riley shifts his shoulders before maneuvering his way over to the bed and flopping down on it. "That's probably a good idea. Try the fifteenth floor."

"The old obstacle course floor?" Colt asks.

Riley stretches his legs out. "Yes, they haven't been using it and they rarely send any guards down there because that is where all of the Undesirables took refuge."

I smile, remembering the obstacle course and Mom and Gretel's visits. How we all worked together; the SCs, the Undesirables, the princess and her nanny, Miss Brita. Fun times! The princess was happy down there, we all were. Will we ever be happy again?

"Fifteenth floor, it is!" He stretches his arms over his head and hits the ceiling. "We have to find something or we'll kill each other on this trip."

Suma cracks the door open. "Just thought I'd let you know the ship's not leaving on time. They didn't have time to let everyone know. There is a large group of visitors touring the ship so we have to wait for all of them to disembark." She almost shuts the door before adding. "I'm going back up there, but it's a mess. Lots of people milling about."

"Chaos." Colt stretches his arms in front of his chest and knocks into a shelf protruding from the wall. "Sounds as if a Merc like me needs to do some reconnaissance." He opens the door slightly and peers out, before disappearing down the corridor.

I sit on the bed beside Riley. "Brother, looks like it's just me and you now." I tug at my apron and pull off the wooden shoes. "These are cute, but way too difficult to wear all of the time." I rub my feet. It feels good to stretch out my toes.

Riley scoots back on the bed using it as a chair. "What are we going to do for clothes? We can't keep wearing these."

"Wait a minute." I open the door and peer out into the corridor. "There are always clothes to be cleaned." The laundry cart with bags full of clothes from the SCs stands unguarded in the hall. Since one servant gathers the clothes before the other collects, the cart stands in the hall for a while. I grab a couple of bags and duck back in the room. "These clothes are not clean and the fit might be off. Let's hope not too much, but they will have to do. SCs wear a certain kind of clothes when they are not clothed in their native garb." I unclasp my hat, tossing it on the bed. "Like this." I pull out a shirt and pants for me and one for him.

"Shoes?" He pulls his off and lets them clatter to the floor. "You could use these shoes for weapons."

I laugh. I retreat to the bathroom to change. When I emerge, Riley is dressed in the casual clothes.
For the next few minutes, we wiggle our toes and sit without talking. I have to find Mom and Gretel soon. My mind wanders to the Ferris wheel and all its glory. A tear runs down my cheek as I think of the army of children I left behind. I only hope that Aunt Sandra's boys have found them. Sad to think that most of the adults that were once deemed Undesirables probably won't be there when I return. I'm traveling to the unknown, America, but remain strong in my conviction that I will return.

A knock at the door startles us both. "Paisley? Riley?" It's Colt. We crack the door just enough for Colt to squeeze in. "You were right about the fifteenth floor, Riley. I found us a place to hide."

"With more room, I hope." I say.

Riley pulls his legs up on the bed sitting as cross-legged as possible. He looks very uncomfortable. "I'll have to fold myself in half to stay in here any longer with this many people. When can we go?" He leans over to retrieve his shoes and tumbles onto the floor. He hits his shoulder and grimaces. "We also need other shoes. Something needs to be done about these."

We change back into the Holland outfits, but we take the other clothes with us. It is a catch-22, if we wear the comfortable clothes with the clunky shoes we will stand out. We decide that it will be better for each of us to wear the whole outfit, wooden shoes and all.

There is actually an art to sneaking out, not looking like you're sneaking. The three of us try our best to master this.

Colt decides to make it a competition by sprinting down the stairs. Although he is out of sight, I hear him stomping. Riley and I keep up as much as we can while wearing wooden shoes.

Riley clotheslines me with his arm. "Wait." I fall with a thump and he sits beside me and holds a finger to his lips.

"Why?" I whisper.

"Listen."

I strain my ears and I hear voices. I recognize one as Colt. Oh no, he's been found. I whisper to Riley, "What do we do now?" Riley shrugs.

We don't have much time to wait. Colt walks slowly back up the stairs.

Riley and I stand. We see who is shoving him from behind. The SC who turned us in. The one who told all of our secrets. The main reason we were sentenced to die.

Baako, the betrayer.

Chapter 11

Riley jumps in front of me and reaches around Colt to slap Baako on the back. "Hi, Baako. So glad you joined us."

"Huh?" A stunned Baako lets go of Colt's collar. "Is that you, Riley?" Baako makes a scrunched-up face. "What kind of outfit are you wearing? You look like a girl." He points to Riley's feet. "Are those wooden?"

"You won't believe why I have to wear this get up!" Riley lifts his feet. "I can't believe I have to wear these awful shoes. Let me tell you…"

Baako interrupts, "What about these two?" He cuts his eyes at me and my stomach churns. I could knock him in the head and sleep fine tonight.

"Let's go where it's quiet." Riley pushes Baako back, gently guiding him down the stairs. "We can talk on floor thirteen."

Baako hesitates, but relents and goes in front. Riley turns to us for a moment and whispers "Follow my lead."

I shrug and Colt and I follow Riley. I have no idea where we are going or what we are doing, but we really don't have a choice. I think Riley may be going to kill Baako and with what Baako did to me, I'm not that unhappy about that prospect.

Every time I see his face, it brings me back to that time we were set to free all of the enslaved Undesirables and Uncounteds, but Baako told the king of our plan. I feel my face flush with anger. I try to walk without shooting glances full of hate at Baako, but it is hard.

We finally arrive at Floor thirteen. Riley steps out into the corridor and walks to an open room. My heart races with anticipation and fear. I do hate Baako, but I'm not sure I can be a part of whatever Riley has in mind for him. Not sure at all.

We step into a storage room. Large cans of beans, tomatoes, and corn line the shelves on one side. The other side is stacked with boxes of tissue, paper towels, and toilet paper along with bottles of cleaning products.

Riley flips on the overhead bulb and closes the door behind us. He crosses his arms and stares at Baako. "They told you, didn't they?"

Baako looks at Colt and me. "Told me what?"

"I thought so." Riley places his hand on Baako's' shoulder. "I told them you could handle it."

"Handle what?" Baako shakes his head.

Riley crooks his finger, drawing Baako in closer and says in a low voice, "Colt, Paisley, and I have been on a secret mission since..." Riley stops talking and looks at Colt. "How long it's been Colt?"

Colt hesitates then says, "A long time. I can't remember now."

Riley smiles. "That's right. See how long it's been. Not even Colt can remember when it started. What about you Paisley, do you remember when we were recruited?"

I shake my head. I guess Riley is doing a good con job because Baako is wide-eyed and listening intently following every word. It's sad. He's so gullible. No wonder the king and his goons were able to get Baako to tattle on us. He is so naïve he doesn't know when people are telling him the truth or when they are making up a whopper of a lie. Right now, it's the whopper variety.

"What kind of mission?" Baako breathes in.

Yes, he's hooked. Riley spins an intricate story about

how, when he was collecting the harvest at the farms, Colt and I were his secret contacts. We had been placed there as spies to report. For all these years, Riley has always been our contact. When the farms were disbanded, Colt and I were brought back on the ship to infiltrate the Undesirables and the Uncounteds. We had planned to tell the king about the escape plot, but Baako beat us to it.

"Hold it!" Baako stops him and stares at both of us. He crosses his arms defiantly.

For a moment, I think we might have to kill him after all. Then he asks, "Why should I believe you?"

I know the answer to this one—an answer that he'll believe. "Because we're alive. The king made a big thing about killing us. You saw that. Don't you remember the whole *I'm going to execute you two and save the rest?*"

Baako looks up as if he is trying to conjure up that memory. "That's right."

It scares me how good of a liar I am becoming.

Colt joins in. "Why would he leave us alive if we weren't telling the truth?"

I hold my breath. Will Baako believe this whole made up story? It doesn't take long.

He drums his fingers on his lips. "What's your new mission?"

I shouldn't hate Baako, I should feel sorry for him. He thought he was doing what was best for his family. He really doesn't know what's going on. With all the unrest in the world, it behooves people to know whom they can trust and whom they can't, and when someone is lying. Poor Baako's so dumb, he can't tell the difference

Between the three of us we convince him that Riley and I are disguised as living dolls (SCs), representing Holland to spy on the SCs and make sure the princess is protected. How Colt is now pretending to be a Merc so he can protect the two major and very secret, special relatives of the king, who we describe differently, but who are in fact, my mom and Gretel. I threw that part of the story in. It would give Colt a reason to spend time with Gretel; it would give them some protections while we made the transatlantic trip.

"We have to hide while we're here, Baako, so we'll be living on the fifteenth floor." Riley concludes the pack of lies.

Baako shakes Riley's hand and then mine and Colt's. "Is there anything I can do to help you?"

I pipe up. "It would be easier if you could bring our food every day then we wouldn't have to sneak around."

Baako salutes. "Just have to clear it with Lamar."

"No!" Riley shouts. "Lamar can't know! Remember, he was the one who thought you couldn't handle it." Baako nods, then Riley continues, "Besides, just think when we complete our mission and we tell Lamar how much you helped us and..." He salutes Baako in an exaggerated move. "I wouldn't be surprised if you didn't get a promotion out of this."

Baako puffs out his chest. "You really think so?"

We all nod. Baako slaps his knee. "I'll do it. You three just go down to the fifteenth floor and *do not worry* about a thing. I'll make sure you get three squares a day. A promotion?" He grins. "Anything else you need?"

A wry smile crosses Riley's face. "Shoes."

Chapter 12

Baako trots off. I guess to find shoes.

It's funny, seeing him run off so giddy and happy. It's difficult to wait for him to get out of sight before we look at each other and break out in a laugh.

We need to get back on track. Enough of this playing around. "Let's go find Mom and Gretel." I am afraid to wait any longer.

Riley gathers his composure. "With the chaos of everyone trying to get the people on and off the ship, this might be the perfect time to find them." He points to a waiter who rushes by. "Everyone is busy and no one's paying attention."

Colt claps his hands together. "Gretel. You don't have to ask me twice. Let's go, but to the lab first."

I'm okay with seeing Gretel first, if it makes Colt happy. I have to see my family. Now.

The lab is easy to find with Riley's help. We decide to send Colt in first since he is dressed as the Merc.

It's been a half an hour. I'm patiently waiting, but Riley paces back and forth. "What's he doing in there?"

"How would I know?" I crack the door open to peer in.

The door flies open and bonks me in the face. Gretel

rushes out, her face lit up like a child seeing her first Christmas tree or the first time I saw the Ferris wheel lit up. She grabs me. "Colt just told me you were out here! He and I've been sitting in there talking—well doing other things too." She flushes. "Never mind. You don't need to know about that." She throws her arms around me. "But I'm sorry I didn't come out right away." She backs off, as Colt comes through the door. She smacks Colt hard in the face. "I can't believe my sister has been out here the whole time and you didn't tell me." She whacks him one more time in the arm before pulling me into a hug again. "Paisley! We thought you were dead!" Tears stream down her face. "Come in, you two." She moves through the open door into the room.

Colt must have had a good visit. He has a grin on his face reminiscent of a cat with a gut filled with an angler's load of trout. "She couldn't wait a minute longer."

Riley, Colt, Gretel, and I enter the lab. We fill Gretel in about what happened after we left.

"The ambassador's perfected the cure." Gretel smiles. "I like the fact that I helped. It was all with your blood, Paisley."

Colt slaps me on the back. "Glad you have that *special* blood."

Riley shoots his eyes toward me and blinks in a strange way. "She is special in every way." After that comment, he blushes.

Him turning red makes me feel funny. My stomach flip-flops. "Special for getting into trouble." I shift uncomfortably.

Gretel hugs me again tightly. "I wouldn't have it any other way. Enough of this talk."

I love my sister. I especially love her when she reads my mood and knows it is time for her to intervene. At times like this, when she covers for me to make me comfortable in an uncomfortable situation, I love her even more.

The ambassador breaks through the door. He spies me and his face turns ashen. "Paisley? What are you doing here? Being on this ship puts you in great danger." He looks over at Colt. "Both of you."

I stand up and fight the urge to hug my *real* father. No one else knows our secret. "We had to come back. We appreciate you saving us, Ambassador Grayson." It sounds formal, but I'm trying not to give the connection away. "I heard that it was my blood that you used for the cure." The ambassador doesn't say anything so I add, "Don't you want to talk to me about my blood?"

He looks confused for a moment, and then plays along. "Yes, if you could come this way." He glances at Gretel and the boys. "I'll bring her back in a minute. I might need another sample of her blood."

Riley hovers protectively. "You're not going to hurt her, are you?"

Gretel slaps at Riley. "Of course he's not." Riley sits down and the ambassador and I move toward the back of the lab.

When we are safely out of their sight, he pulls me into a hug and kisses my cheek. "Why did you leave the farm? You were safe there." He pushes me out and stares at me as he releases the hug. "You have no idea what I went through to assure your safety."

"I understand, but when I found out the ship was going to America..." I stop, hearing other voices.

He puts his fingers to his lips. "This way."

We walk down a corridor and enter a secluded area. It's an indoor office. The back of the area is stacked with books and has a porthole looking out to the ocean; two of the walls are half-full of marked charts with bookshelves full of books lining the bottom half. The inside wall is made up of the entrance, a door on one side and the other half of the wall is part wall and part windows with opened blinds. The office is full of papers strewn about in no logical organizational pattern. Two rolling chairs are stacked high.

This looks just like him. Brilliant, but unorganized. He is an exceptional scientist, but probably the only person in the world who understands how his own mind works. I can see a small part of that in me. It makes me smile that a part of my father has found its way into me though we weren't together during my childhood years. He peers out of the inside windows. He closes the blinds and shuts the door. "We won't be disturbed in here."

"How did you find out about America? Have you been leaving the farm?" He asks. "Sit." He points to a rolling chair. "Might need to move a few things."

I roll the lab chair toward me. "We had people going out to scout the newspapers and media so we could keep up with what was going on."

He picks up the papers off the stool and moves them to yet another pile on the counter. "Who else was with you on the farm?"

"The Undesirables. They followed our horse and buggy." I stop for a moment and sit. "I think their plan was to save us. So sweet." I sigh, thinking about our army of children back on the farm. It makes me both happy and sad at the same time.

"I cannot protect you on this ship." He empties his chair and sits. It is noisy, rolling across the plastic guard on the floor. He moves beside me and grabs my hand.

I jerk my hand out of his. "I'm not asking you to." My face flushes. Why does everyone think I have to have someone to watch over me? Colt, Riley and now my father.

"I didn't mean to make you angry." He leans back. "I'm just worried."

I stand and pick up an empty test tube from the counter and roll it in my hands. "You should be the one worried. I heard rumor that they have my brother, my real brother, your son, held hostage so you will do what the king wants." I stop, watching him to get a glimmer of a reaction so I'll know if it's the truth. The ambassador flinches.

I shout, "So it's true!"

He stands up and takes the test tube out of my hand motioning for me to sit back down, which I do. He takes a deep breath. "Yes."

I jump up again. "We need..."

He pulls me back down into the chair. "No, you don't *need* to do anything. You *need* to keep out of sight until we get to Orlando. I can't help you on the ship, but I can do a lot for you in America. I'll help your brother too. Hide until then. I have a plan."

I start to ask him about this plan, but there will be plenty of time for that. I want to know other things. "You never told me his name."

He frowns. "Whose name?"

I let out a frustrated gasp. "My brother."

He smiles. "Your brother's name is Oliver."

"Is my name really Paisley?" I ask.

He takes my hand in his. "It is now, but you were born with the name Penelope. Your mother was a big fan of *The Odyssey*."

I smile and sit back with a big sigh, causing the chair to roll. There is something about knowing my real name, even though I'll never use it.

"What was my mother like?"

"She was one of a kind. You are like her in many ways. She was always the first to fight for what she thought was right." His eyes gleam. "She was a brilliant scientist in her own right."

"She was?"

He pats my hair. "Yes, you probably have inherited her brains. I know your brother has. He is young, but he is a genius with communications. They have him working to restore all of the communications for the world. He is the expert in that field and he's only fourteen." He sighs and taps my head. "Of course, I know that if you'd been given the schooling your brother had been given all throughout your life you would probably have been working right by his side." He smiles. "It makes me smile to think of my children working together on something. Your mother took care of us. She was the heart of our family. I see a lot of her in you, especially your eyes. You have the same eyes."

It's nice to know that about my mother and realize we share the same color eyes, but it also makes me realize that she was just my birth mother. Without her, I wouldn't be here, but my mother and my sister are my real family. I must always remember that.

My father and I talk about what my mother was like and life on the military base and a little about America. It all sounds wonderful, but of course, the stories were all from before the virus. He is so animated, reliving the stories I realize how much life has been sucked out of him by these piranhas he calls family now. His wife, the queen and her father, the king.

"Did you get enough of her blood?" Riley calls out.

"I think you have a bodyguard." My father opens a cabinet and pulls out a sticky bandage and puts it across the inside crook of my elbow. "For show."

I press the edges of the bandage down. "In here."

I hug my father one last time before I depart.

We decide to give Colt a few alone minutes with Gretel to say a proper good-bye. I have to admit I've never seen my sister so happy. Her eyes glisten when she looks at Colt. Love is written all over her. I think it's great that in the midst of all of this turmoil and death the two of them have found each other. It makes me hopeful that one day I will find my own Colt.

As we exit, I look over at Colt. "Now, onto Mom?"

He nods.

Once again, Riley is able to maneuver throughout the passages with ease and finds the short cut to the kitchen. In order to reach the kitchen we have to travel to the top deck. People are scurrying about. The ship hasn't left port yet, but most of the ship's inhabitants seem to be on the top deck. The elite leisurely stroll the deck occasionally barking orders at the servants as they scurry about trying to obey or anticipate the ones in charge's every whim. Not knowing how much time we have before the ship leaves, we try to hurry.

Finally, we walk into the kitchen. It's chaos. Cooks are emptying trays of food and pulling baking sheets out of the oven. We travel through the entire kitchen and at first, no one takes any kind of notice of us.

I spy my mother frosting a cake. "Mom!"

Mom turns and drops the spatula she is holding. It clangs to the floor. People fall silent for a moment before returning to their chores. She bursts into tears and grabs me. "Oh Paisley! I just knew you weren't dead. I could feel it. I would know if you were dead. I'm so glad. Oh, Paisley!"

Our crying and hugging garner the attention of a couple of workers, who are basting a turkey on the counter next to

Mom. One of the workers chastises, "You need to be quiet. We have work to do."

Mom pushes us toward the back door and swings it open. "In here. There will be a little more privacy. No one is in here right now. This is clean up."

"I missed you, Mom." We spend the next few minutes telling her about how we planned to get her and Gretel off, but how we didn't have time because the ship is leaving early.

"Now we're stuck going to America with you and Gretel."

She hugs me again. "Together, but you'd better make sure that you don't run into the royals or any of the Mercs that know you two or Riley. Be careful."

"I promise." I hug her again. "We will be on the fifteenth floor."

I don't want to leave her. My heart is filled. I'm home. Home is here.

I memorize my mother's smile as we take off out the doors.

By the time we get back to the fifteenth floor, we can feel the ship's movement and the scurrying is down to a minimum, sure signs that we are on our way across the Atlantic Ocean heading to America. I don't know if that's a good thing or a bad thing.

Riley laughs as we shut the door behind us. Sitting in the middle of the floor are two pairs of camel colored leather everyday shoes, one for me and one for Riley.

Baako came through.

Chapter 13

Ten days is a long time to hide on a ship, but we try to make the best of it. It only takes one day for Riley and me to figure out the schedule. We have six hours in the daytime when most of the SCs are busy with their child owners. It seems that the rich like to laze around in the morning. We have not run across one of the royals or any of the Mercs in the early hours. The Mercs must stay up late keeping order when the wealthy are awake. I love it. Special moments for ourselves. We use this time to gather food, visit Gretel in the lab, and Mom in the kitchen. I even find a few minutes every day to sit and have a coffee with my father.

Riley and I are thrown together daily because of our Dutch SC status. It makes it more believable if we travel as one unit. I haven't been alone with Riley this much and I enjoy it. So much of my life has been bringing in harvest. Now that I've experienced it, playing is an activity that I look forward to.

"How about a game of shuffleboard?" He says one morning. I had never heard of shuffleboard before this trip, but here we are playing it daily and quite competitively too. Riley wins handily at first, but I catch on later, even beating him a few times. We work out in the gym. It seems silly to me since I have always gotten all of my exercise doing chores on the farm, but I go anyway, enjoying the treadmill the most. Laughing at the idea that I need a machine to help me run. We play a few games in the bowling alley and the crazy golf course.

"Stole you something today." Riley holds up a piece of cloth no larger than my arm.

I grab the blue polka-dotted fabric out of his hand. "What is it, a hat?"

He holds up a pair of underwear looking things. "No, it's a bathing suit. I got one too."

I frown. "Why do I need a bathing suit? Are we going to swim to America?"

He points to a closet door labeled "Women." "No silly, we're going to swim in a pool. Go in there and change." He hands over a white piece of meshy fabric. "This is called a cover-up. Put it over your suit. There is a heated pool on the third deck."

I shrug, holding up the suit and cover up. I'm not really sold, but I am willing to try.

I emerge in a few minutes, tugging the meshy white shirt over the bathing suit. I feel naked. Riley stands there in the swim trunks and shirt. I look away. The sight of him tingles something strange inside of me. Maybe it's because we've spent so much time together, but the thought of not seeing Riley every day makes me sad. Not seeing him would be as if a piece of me wasn't here. I try to concentrate on something else. Like his feet. Thanks goodness he's wearing his other shoes. The wooden ones I am wearing look ridiculous with the swimsuit. I smile when he hands me regular ones. He thinks of everything.

We travel to the third floor and I follow as he leads me into a large enclosed room with an inviting pool. The water is the most beautiful turquoise. It is like a large tub and the water is just as warm. The swim is wonderful. There are no other people there.

"Our own private island," he says.

I continue with the fantasy. "We are rich and off for our exotic getaway at the island of..."

"Paisley and Riley," he finishes.

I giggle. "Not very original, but okay—the Island of Paisley and Riley. I like it that you put my name first."

"I always put you first." His eyes gleam.

I jump in the water. What he said makes me happy and uncomfortable all at the same time.

Colt has the run of the ship, as long as he stays out of Lamar's view. It's nice how Baako is helping with this. Baako has completely bought into being one of the king's secret spies. He warns us when Lamar is close, and checks on Mom and Gretel daily since he thinks they are long lost relatives of the king and royalty in their own right. We had to fill Mom and Gretel in on it, since the first time he saw Gretel, he bowed.

"Don't bow," I told him. "You'll get them killed by the royals' enemies." Every day he brings Mom and Gretel extras such as food that he confiscates from the royals.

Between what news Colt gets and Baako slipping us information, we keep apprised of the daily happenings in the outside world. It is that knowledge that is the most disturbing. We read stories of the dissidents and their raids on harvest stockpiles and the growing unpopularity of democracy. There is a strict censorship on the news. A powerful machine spins every story to sway the populace the king's way. The ambassador *may not* be safe on the ship. I don't know why I have such a bad feeling about that, but I fear for my father's life.

Day four, I meet with my father for our daily coffee in his office.

"I think your brother Oliver is being held at what used to be a theme park in Orlando," my father confides. "That is where I will head first when the ship docks. I want you to come with me. I have a group of supporters who will hide both you and him until the election is over."

"What about you?" I take a sip of coffee.

He picks up a square of sugar. "Sugar?"

He knows I cannot resist sugar. I slide my cup over for him to drop in the cube, which begins to dissolve as soon as it hits the coffee. "I can't go and walk out on Colt, Riley, and my family. Not even for my brother." I ask again, "What about you?"

He stirs his coffee and leans back. "I can't abandon the cause especially since my wife is pregnant." He pauses. "I will just be able to work better knowing my children are safe."

"We aren't your only children."

He takes a sip and then sets the coffee cup on the table. "I know, but the princess is being taken care of and the queen is not due for months."

"How is the queen?"

He picks the coffee back up. "She's having a difficult time. I am afraid the virus medication that I gave her early in the pregnancy—the same virus inoculation that I gave you as a child and your mother when she was pregnant with your brother—has had an adverse effect on her." He holds his coffee chin high, not drinking. "I didn't realize that because she already had the immunity, from eating the herbs on her island, that it would make her so sick."

I pat his knee. "You couldn't have known."

"True." He drinks. "Tests show that the baby is fine."

"Do you know what it is—boy or girl?"

"Boy." He smiles. "I will have two of each. You, your brother, now the princess, and this little one. You have a big family, Paisley."

It is a big secret family, one that I cannot reveal for fear of death. I feel sorry for my father, caught in the middle of this war, and in the middle of two families. Of course, I can identify because I have three families now. The one I was born to, my father, my brother, and my half-sister—the one I grew up with, Gretel and my mom—and the family that isn't related but has become my family, Colt, Riley, and the army of children at our Ferris wheel farm. For someone who grew up so alone, the space in my world has suddenly filled up. Not sure if that is a good thing or not.

Chapter 14

Days five through nine on the ship are uneventful. Day ten, land is sighted. That morning, we go through the same schedule. Riley and I wait until mid-morning, while Colt goes out early in his Merc outfit to scout the ship.

Riley and I are still in the room when Colt returns. "Something's going on in the lab."

"Gretel?" I ask. "Is anything wrong with Gretel?" I start for the door. "What about the ambassador?"

Colt grabs my arm to stop me from leaving. "It doesn't seem to have anything to do with Gretel. They had a crew in there taking all of the ambassador's stuff."

"What stuff?" I ask.

Colt searches for words. "You know, his papers, files, test tubes."

Riley leans up against the wall with his hand. "Was the ambassador there? The king? Lamar?"

Colt presses his head between his hands. "Wait a minute. Too many questions." He takes a big breath. "Lamar wasn't there. The king wasn't either. There was some talk about the cure and the virus. All I can tell you is that the ambassador was going ape-crazy and yelling that he would never try to hurt his own child or his wife."

I cross my arms. "They think he did something to his pregnant wife?" I look at Riley. "That's crazy!"

Riley nods. "It's possible the king is beginning a case to discredit him before we land in America. It would make sense that they would want an article that paints him in an unfavorable light. They want to hurt his credibility. They want to discredit him. I heard the king is worried. The ambassador is too popular in America and now he's gaining popularity in Europe. That's dangerous for anyone who does not want democracy."

"Stop for a minute and answer my question." I jerk up. "Tell me. Who said he hurt his wife?"

"It doesn't matter." Colt interrupts, "I'm worried about Gretel." He opens the outside door. "I'm going to the lab. You two worry about the politics."

I watch Colt leave and then turn my attention to Riley. "Should we go to the lab?"

Riley says, "No, not with the Mercs there. Colt will make sure they are okay. Let's wait until it's all clear. And I really don't know who said the ambassador hurt his wife."

"Thanks. Promise that we'll check on everyone later."

Riley nods.

I am worried too. Although the one thing I shouldn't worry about is Gretel with Colt checking on her. That's a better job for someone pretending to be a Merc than for me or Riley pretending to be SCs.

"I don't want to stay here." I ask, "Where can we go?"

Riley shrugs. "We're all packed here. I guess we can walk the decks and see if we can figure out exactly when the ship is going to dock. After we know everyone is fine, are we going to try to get off, or lay low while we are at the dock?"

"I'm not sure. I guess we can walk up there and see what's going on. Want to?" I ask.

"Sure, why not?" Riley opens the outside door. "It won't hurt anything. And to make certain, we can dress in these adorable outfits." He pulls out his Holland garb. "I'll even wear the shoes just to make sure we are covered if we get spotted."

He pulls on the wooden shoes.

I smile. "You can always use them as weapons."

After changing, we take our time ascending. The top deck is a bustle of movements. Waiters balance trays full of drinks on their hands, offering beverages to the elegantly clothed patrons, while other waiters fill their trays with empty glasses.

"Over here." Riley pulls a couple of chairs to the side. "I think we can sit here incognito."

I look around. "We might not be able to see anything." I smile, sit, and crouch to peer through the gates. "If I scrunch down, I can see everything that happens."

"You let me know if you see something interesting." Riley sits and stretches his legs in front of him, kicking off the wooden shoes. "I'm going to enjoy the fresh air. Don't you miss the outdoors?" He rubs his feet. "We've been inside the belly of this ship way too long." He takes a deep breath. "Fresh air, I miss fresh air."

"You're right!" I lean back in my chair and take in a deep breath. "It's great!"

He grabs my hand. "We can pretend we are a wealthy couple. Here on our..." He winks at me. "Our honeymoon."

I laugh. Normally, I might have knocked him in the arm or said no, but somehow it doesn't bother me that he mentioned honeymoon and me in the same sentence. I remember when I first met him, he seemed so skinny. I don't know if it's because he's grown up a little or...I guess I don't know what it is, but he seems so handsome now.

I hold his hand. We sit there for a while. It's nice.

"I don't understand why I am going to jail. What's going to happen to all of my research?" The ambassador's voice booms from below. "That research is important! Don't you understand?"

I peer over the edge to the scene unfolding below. Four Mercs surround the ambassador. The king stands in front of him and bellows, "My daughter is ill. You have given her medicine that made her sick. I'm not sure you didn't do that on purpose."

"I didn't!" The ambassador pushes his glasses up on his nose. "Why would I hurt my own wife? My unborn baby boy?"

The king waves his scepter in a dismissive way. "I don't care what you say; she is sick and until she is well you will be incarcerated. You'll be transported to jail as soon as we land in America."

The ambassador holds his palms together. "Please let me out. I have to present to the members of the Consortium of the World. I have to argue for democracy. I have to let them know that I have found a cure for the virus and that I plan to give it to every man, woman and child for free." He bows to the king. "These things are important. Our world will be better when I do this. Please my king, I must finish my mission. I've sacrificed so much."

The king jerks his scepter and slams it into the ambassador's chest. "You have sacrificed nothing. You have lived like a wealthy man. I have given you my only daughter as your wife. You have gotten a state-of-the-art lab. I have given you everything you want." He clenches the edges of his robe in his hands. "How do you repay me? You make my daughter ill and you refuse to give me the formula to your new vaccination even though it is my wealth and power that made it possible." The king slams down his scepter. "You want to give everything away. You want my daughter and me and even *your* daughter to live like paupers. I will not allow that to happen." He presses the scepter into the ambassador's chest. "Don't you forget who is king. Ambassador Grayson, you are hereby placed under arrest. You will be transferred to a prison cell when we port. That is all."

I jump up from my hiding place, leaving Riley sitting. "No, you can't!"

Everyone stops and looks at me. I peer up at Riley, who makes a move to follow me. I shake my head slightly, begging him not to move. I realize too late, I have made a bad mistake. My only hope is that Colt and Riley won't be caught so there is someone out there who might be able to rescue me from my own idiot reactions.

"Help," I whisper to myself. I clutch my bullet clover necklace. "Find me a way out of this."

The king's eyes train on me.

Chapter 15

The king walks around me. My father holds his breath. I hold mine. I expect Riley is holding his breath too.

The king stops in front of me. "You look familiar. Do I know you?"

I try to disguise my voice by speaking Dutch while keeping my words to a minimum. "No."

The king's eyes narrow. "I've met you before. Just can't think of where."

It's not a question so I don't answer.

The king shakes his head. No way out of this or at least no scenarios that I play in my head that end with me and my father being released unharmed. I don't think my father has breathed a complete breath since I found my way down here.

King Ahomana says, "Why do you care about what I do with the ambassador?"

I shrug, trying to buy time to come up with a good answer. What would make sense? Absolutely nothing comes in my mind.

I open my mouth to spew some kind of nonsense I hope that the king won't be able to understand when I hear a voice from behind me shout. "*Her*, that girl. She can tell you about me."

I turn. Standing in all of her glory is the woman who talked to me when I sneaked onto the ship with her group. I try to recall what we discussed as we squeezed in during the tour. I can't remember.

"What do you need me to tell them?" I ask her in my best Dutch accent.

She says, "She's the Holland representative. The tour..." She pauses looking to me to fill in the name of the tour.

I don't know the name of the tour so I fake it with nonsense talk. "Yes, we were on our way with our guide and he was telling us about all the wonderful things about the king and..." I run out of things to say. I can only hope that the king's vanity will kick in and he won't look too closely at me.

The navy blue suited woman completes my sentence, "Then the ship started moving and we were caught on it with no security papers or anything. Right, dearie?"

I nod. "Yes that's right and we've been..." I wait again for her to fill it in. Might as well let her. She's doing a great job. If the king buys all this bull.

"Yes, we've been or at least *I* have been, at the mercy of kind servants ever since. What about you, dear? How did you make it for these ten days?" The woman asks.

"Same as you," I lie.

King Ahomana waves his scepter. "Enough of this nonsense. Both of you leave my sight. Your chatter bores me." He glares at me. "You will not interrupt your king again. Do you understand?"

I bow and back away. I finally hear my father let a breath go and begin to breathe regularly. The only thing I accomplished was not being thrown in jail along with my father. But what can I do to help him? I'll ask Riley. Maybe between the two of us we can come up with a plan.

I separate quickly from the suited woman to make sure she doesn't continue our conversation and waste no time making my way back to the deck. Riley jerks me down beside him by one arm in the hiding place and hugs me. "Quit doing stuff like that! You're going to get yourself killed."

Tears flow. Guess I was more scared than I thought. I bury my head in his shoulder. I must look like an idiot, tightly crouched in an almost fetal position bawling my eyes out. "Sorry," I mumble.

He rubs my hair. "Some of us would miss you if you got thrown in jail." He lifts my chin and forces a soft chuckle. "You wouldn't be there long though. You'd talk someone into freeing you."

I dry my tears. "I would, wouldn't I?"

He nods.

I peer over just in time to see the Mercs haul off my father. "What *are* we going to do about the ambassador?"

"Not sure there's much we can do." Riley shrugs. "We could get off the ship and try to find out where they are holding him, but that is a dangerous choice." He stands up. "How would we ever get back on the ship? You *do* want to return to Bavaria, right?"

He pulls me to my feet and I stand beside him. "Of course, it's just…"

Riley knocks into me with his shoulder. "You want to save them all." He reaches his arm around my waist. "It's one of your best traits."

Riley likes some of my traits. I smile. His arm around my waist makes me all tingling inside. Before, I felt the same about Colt and Riley, like they were my brothers. Now it's different; if this were a race, Riley would win.

He moves his arm. "We'd better go below before we *really* do get caught."

I rest my elbows on the railing. "Just a while longer. Look, you can see land. We should dock soon. Can't we stay up here and at least *see* America even if we're not going to be able to touch it?"

He slips his arm back around my waist. "Guess it can't hurt anything."

It takes about an hour to get close enough to make out anything but outlines. I try to imagine what I think this world looked like before the twelve years of deterioration. I cradle my hand over my eyes like a sailor I once saw in a picture. I try to look as far as I can see. No hills, mountains, or rises of any sort. Seems strange that they can actually call this land, since it is so flat. The only protrusions are buildings taking the place of mountains, clumped together densely and standing proudly. I read somewhere that this once was a bustling metropolis of people, art, and business. The skyline is now consigned to serve as a reminder of how desolate, quarantined, and sad our world has become. I think of our army of children waiting patiently back home on the farm. Standing erect and ready to pounce on this new world, fighting, scratching and clawing, whatever it takes to mold the future into something they can be proud of.

It takes about fifteen minutes for the ship to maneuver for docking. The crew shouts orders to each other. I am amazed at how well they work together to bring the magnificent beast to a standstill.

Riley and I are quiet for a while. I enjoy standing with his arm around my waist. Makes me feel normal. Like two friends on a cruise, waiting to disembark. How funny! Nothing farther from the truth.

It's a few more minutes before they lower the gangplank. I'm jealous. I wish I could get off the ship. I want to see America. I long to travel to Orlando, where all your dreams come true. How awful to get this close yet not be able to get off the ship.

I sigh. It hurts to watch. I pull away from Riley's arm. I stand knowing I need to make my way down the stairs, but for some reason I am unable to move.

After a few more moments, my senses return and I ask, "Riley, you ready?"

His eyes are sunken and sad. "I guess we really should go find Colt. He might have been looking for us."

"That's true." I haven't thought of Colt all morning, or Mom, or Gretel, or even Baako. **The ambassador's fate has been the only thing on my mind.**

A few workers leave the ship first. A couple of minutes later, I see my father being led away by a group of Mercs. I assume he is being taken to jail. Will I ever see him again? That thought blows through my mind and for a moment, the loss makes me sadder than I have ever been in my life. Why do they feel the need to surround him with such burly men? What's he going to do, run away? I watch, unable to move. He is taken to a waiting car, shoved in, and the car disappears from my sight.

It must have been my distress that made me let my guard down and not be aware of my surroundings. After ten days hiding on the ship, I turn and face the one person who could blow my cover to smithereens.

The princess.

Chapter 16

"Miss Paisley! Miss Paisley!" The four-year-old breaks from her companion's grip and dashes toward me. What can I do? Absolutely nothing. If this is my last act, I'll make it a good one. She's my sister, even if she doesn't know it. I reach down and hug her tight. My cover is totally blown now. I let out a long sigh; one of resolution.

I grit my teeth and plant my feet. I know in my heart one thing and that is that I do not give up. Ever!

I shoot Riley a quick look and mouth, "Stay. Don't follow me." I pull off the wooden shoes, hug them to my body, and take off running.

The princess thinks it's a game. She trails behind me. "I run too!" She yells, giggling. "Wait, Miss Paisley! Wait for me!"

In a flash, we are surrounded by Mercs. Fortunately for me, the princess's safety is more important than my escape. While the princess unknowingly runs block for me, I safely sprint across the plank onto the American shore.

What now? I have no idea. I'm completely alone. I dash across the shipyard, dodging the myriad of workers. I use them as cover, occasionally glancing back over my shoulder, half-expecting to see a Merc hot on my trail. None, so far. I sprint, no idea who is chasing me, or what I am running to, gasping for breath.

I heave, fall to my knees, and throw up breakfast. I look for cover. I'm still clinging to the wooden shoes. I might need them later and I don't want to leave any clues behind.

There are many structures. I choose one. There is a large rolling door at the entrance and I push it up just enough for me to roll under before sliding it back closed. I hope this will give me a few minutes to hide. Basically, the building is a huge roof over water. Boats are tied up with wood docks surrounding them. A few large water vessels hang from the rafters tied up and forgotten. It makes me think of a graveyard. A graveyard for boats that were once used for fun and now dust covers their once pristine hulls, who knows maybe their owners didn't survive the outbreak. There is a walkway in the middle of the dock with stairs leading to an office. A boat covered with a shiny yellow tarp catches my eye—it's big like a yacht. It's hoisted and tied up to the top of the roof, impossible to get to on foot. The good thing about it is it seems unreachable. That's the kind of hiding place I need. If I can figure a way on the hoisted yacht and use the tarp as covering, I might have a fighting chance. I know that shouldn't be a good thing, but it is. I will have to be creative in order to heave myself on board. It's so high, maybe no one will think to search there. I look around for other options. None comes to mind.

The first hurdle is to reach it. A rope, all I need is a rope. I search through some boxes on the dock—no luck.

A little higher starting point might give me more of an opportunity to pull myself up to it. I need a rope. I climb the stairs to the office, scanning the large shelter. No sign of a rope. So much for that idea. I wonder if I can jump it. I back up. No. It's impossible. I don't have enough space to get a running start. I run down a couple of stairs and hear shouting. The Mercs are closing in. No way out! I have to hide now!

I turn the knob on the office door. It's unlocked. Finally, a break! I examine my surroundings and quickly locate a box large enough for me to crouch in. They'll most likely search it, but what choice did I have? I open the latched lid and there sits the most beautiful sight I've ever seen. A rope. I sling it over my shoulder and shut the lid. I glance around, making sure I haven't disturbed anything in the room.

I knot the end of the rope and throw it like a lasso around a beam in the ceiling. The shouts get louder. First try, I miss. Oh no! I throw it again. It falls back down to me! I toss it as hard as I can. Almost! I will be able to think of that *almost* while I'm sitting in jail. Desperate, I heave it again. It hangs for a moment, but falls again! I hear the Mercs right outside the door. I'm running out of time. I toss the rope as hard as I can and at last, it catches. I take my time inching the rope up so it will come down the other side. Finally, I get both sides of the rope together. I tie the ends together. I shimmy up the rope. It reminds me of scaling my Ferris wheel's prong. I make my way to the edge of the yacht's cover. I hold onto the edge making sure I have a hold of the boat and not just the yellow covering. I heave myself up. The entry door begins to slide open. I untie the rope quickly and drag it to me. I lift the cover and slide in the rope. I flatten myself inside the boat. I haul the tarp over me. I hear the access door thump signaling that it is fully open.

I hold my breath. Booted footsteps thud.

A voice yells, "Any sign of her? Search the office!"

Another voice asks, "What about the boats?"

The first voice answers, "Search them all!"

My heart sinks. I hear covers being thrown off. Metal clangs. I shut my eyes and try to imagine how strewn the boat shed is now. I clutch my four-leaf clover necklace hoping to compel its luck to me now. I roll my head to the side and force myself to focus on something, anything. I spot a blue stuffed toy. It looks like the whales I've seen pictures of in books. Maybe this was a child's toy. Might have been left on from before the virus, when everyone took boats out for fun. I blank the noise and slow my breath. All I think about is the toy.

A voice breaks my concentration. "What about this one?" Are they talking about my hiding place? I hold my breath.

"Can't get to it!"

"Are you sure?" The first voice asks.

One of the Mercs yells, "I can try to jump." *Thump!* I

could have told him that wouldn't work. The boat shifts a little as two or more of the Mercs bang on the sides of the boats, taunting, "Come out girlie! Come out if you're in there!"

I concentrate once again on the whale.

A voice yells, "Let's move to another building. She's not here!" Booted footsteps sound before I hear the entrance door come down. I wait. The voices disappear.

I wait a little longer before I stir. I decide to search the yacht for items I might need later. I tiptoe gingerly because the boat rocks slightly with my every movement. I enter through the outside door to explore the living quarters. Inside the cabin, I discover an area that looks like it hasn't been touched for years. I could only surmise that this yacht was left when the virus ravaged and the owners either died or were quarantined. The beds are stripped and sheets and blankets stored. I open the cabinets and find them filled with canned goods and various staples. I stumble upon a box of fruit bars. I pull one out and eat it while I go through the rest of the drawers. The fruity smell's overwhelming. Tickling my taste buds, it's delicious. Guess these things last forever. I can't stay here too long. But I need to be smart and wait long enough to use the darkness as cover. I find a wind up clock and set it one hour. I need some sleep so I can think a little straighter before I figure out my next move. I have no idea where I'll go or how I'll get home or what will happen to Riley or Colt.

For the first time on this journey, I'm completely on my own. Scary!

Chapter 17

I nap for an hour. Afterwards my mind is clearer. I'll organize first then try for some more sleep. I find a backpack and load it full of fruit and cereal bars. I gather a clean shirt, a pair of socks, and a large pair of sneakers. I change into these, hoping to blend in more with this culture than I did before with the Holland outfit. I stuff my Holland outfit and shoes in the backpack. I also find soap, deodorant, shampoo, a flashlight, and a pocketknife. I cut off the end of the sneakers with the pocketknife to make them shorter. I don't have a choice; I have to make them fit me somehow. A baseball cap completes my ensemble. I'm able to stuff my hair underneath it. I disguise my appearance as best I can. An advantage that might become useful. I guess at the time and set the alarm for 0200. Everyone should be asleep by then. Should be safe to leave.

When I wake up, I take my time knotting the rope and shimmying down. I carefully untie the rope and sling it over my shoulder.

Sneaking out of the boat shelter is not as difficult as shimmying down the rope. I throw the rope in my pack for later. I find an unlocked door on the side of the shed and walk out. I have no plan except to get as far away from the ship as possible. I make a mental note of how to find my way back should that need arise. It makes me feel better just knowing where the "Queen Nalani" ocean liner is located. Nothing good has happened on board that ocean cruiser, but it's my connection to home. Or maybe it's the fact that Riley, Colt, Mom, and Gretel are on board making that ship my pseudo home for now.

The shipyard is deserted except for an occasional sentry. I see no one searching for me. I take my time, not wanting to draw attention to my movements. A few shards of sunlight illuminate the area with just enough light for me to attempt escape. I scan for sentries as I look for a way out.

The boats hanging from the rafters and floating in the slips provide no accessible place to hide as I travel through. Fortunately, a few rusted cars speckle the area, enough to use as cover. One harbors a nest of birds that scatter when I walk by. I stop for a moment to see if the movement perked the interest of the guards.

Still unnoticed, I sneak toward the place with the biggest cluster of lights. The only road in or out is guarded. A line of delivery trucks awaits their turn to be given the all clear to leave the compound. It's now or never. I creep up beside a truck with lots of crates in the back. It stinks like garbage. A truck full of fish. Not fresh fish; it's the garbage. Heads, guts, and lots of blood. Decaying fish. I shake my head, hold my nose, and shimmy over the side of the truck bed. I hope that it's a smart move, but certainly not a pleasant one. I dig deep in the smelly fish. If this stench doesn't kill me, I should be fine. No way anyone is going to look through here. I have no way of knowing where this truck is going, but I will let myself be taken as far as it drives or until it delivers this garbage of fish and me.

After the truck clears the gate, I try to find a hole for my nose. The fresh air helps a little. I concentrate on my Ferris wheel. No way to make a plan. I am in a foreign country with no help, riding to who knows where. It's probably not the best decision, but jail as an alternative definitely was not a better choice. No way for me to judge time or how fast we are going. I am completely and totally lost.

Sadness takes over and I have a good long cry. It has a releasing effect on me. Afterwards, I decide to trust that the universe will give me an idea of what to do next.

After many hours, the truck stops. I creep down farther into the fish. I listen.

"Garbage pickup." A man's voice says. The truck starts to move again.

Shortly, the truck stops and the driver slams the door. I peek out; he disappears inside a building. I seize my chance, heave myself over the truck bed, and creep into the shadows.

This area looks like a drop off and pick up point. I put on my backpack and slink out, trying not to be noticed. It might work here since my surroundings reek and I stink of fish. Once I get to a less smelly area, my stench will give away my whereabouts.

It doesn't take long before I'm noticed. A couple of men stack boxes in front of me. One of them looks at me. "Hey are you the new loader?"

I must look like a worker. I fit in here. Filthy, with my hair stuffed in my cap and wearing these disheveled jeans and cotton shirt. But the big giveaway is the pair of cut-off sneakers on my feet. How poor does that appear?

I shrug. Another stands with hands on one side of a box. I figure it won't hurt me, so I grab the other end. For the next hour, I haul boxes. Maybe I can keep hiding as a box loader for a while until I figure out what to do next.

"What's your name, boy?" A man with blackened, broken teeth asks.

I look around and spy a box with the name *Sara Lee* on it. In the lowest voice I can muster I say, "Lee."

The man smiles his non-toothy grin. "Lee, you're a good worker. Were you just purchased?"

Another of the men says, "They like to buy the young strong ones. They last longer."

I nod and grunt out an affirmative answer. We are in America and people are still being bought, still owned. Human trafficking is alive and well in this part of the world too. Unfair and unacceptable! The reality checks as a good reminder about what all of this is about. Bringing about change.

It seems like hours before a man in better clothes stands on the stairs and yells, "Quitting time! Make your way to the grub hall. Eat first, and then get a bath and change of clothes."

The thought of a bath is welcomed since I reek of fish. I follow the bunch into the grub hall. A large pot steams with what smells like fish soup. If I weren't so hungry, I would have passed. I sit at the end of the table with the other three. I wolf down my food. After we toss our used plates on a stainless steel cart, I am led to a table heaped with clothes. The clothes aren't new, but they are clean and smell a lot better than the ones I'm wearing. I gather a pair that appears small hoping they will come close to fitting.

"Lee, get you a better pair of shoes. Those you have are going to make your feet sore." One of my group advises.

I pick out a pair, hold them up to the back of my foot for size, and add them to my pile. Next, I follow them to the showers.

Ut-oh I'm in trouble. They are all showering in the same big stall.

Chapter 18

It's a large shower stall full of men. I avert my eyes. The men are all faced to the middle with their backs to me, and no one is paying attention to anyone except themselves. This is not going to work for me. I'm in trouble.

One of my group members pulls off his shirt. "Here, Lee." He hands me a bar of soap. "Don't be shy. I know, it's strange. It took some getting used to—showering with everyone."

I hold my palms up and he stops undressing. "I can't." My voice is high. I forgot to go low. Fear shoots through my body. I shake.

The three of them surround me outside the showers. Fortunately, they are all still mostly clothed.

"C'mon Lee." One of the men grabs my cap. "It isn't that bad." He smiles, rocking the hat back and forth on my head. "You're one of our crew now. We'll take care of you. Nobody will bother you. Just throw your old clothes in a pile. They'll be thrown away later."

I don't move. "What's your name?" I ask him.

"Sam," he replies.

"Sam, can I trust you?" I say.

Even though Sam is the one I asked, all three nod. I crouch down so as not to let others see. I pull my hat off, letting the hair fall down to my shoulders. "I don't belong here. I'm a girl."

Sam gasps. "Ned, they're buying girls for work now." He looks over at the other two men. He pushes my hat back to my head. "Put that back on while we figure this out."

The three talk in whispers. "She reminds me of my daughter." "We have to protect her." "We can't let them have her." The voices run together. I can't tell who is talking, but they seem to want to help. I hope so. I have to trust them. I have no choice.

Ned holds my shoulders. "We can help you tonight. There's a separate shower on the side. We'll take you there. After that, we can probably only hide you for a couple of days. We need to get you into the underground."

"Underground?"

Ned continues, "We'll explain later." The three men push me into an alcove in the showering area while they finish showering. It's a few more minutes before all is quiet.

Sam says, "You should be able to take a shower undisturbed now. We'll keep watch just in case."

I nod and sneak to the separate stall and shower. Carefully, I make sure that the four-leaf clover necklace stays on my neck. I change into the clean clothes and disguise myself as best as I can. I follow them out to the sleeping quarters. A bunch of men are haphazardly stretched out on the ground on makeshift beds of blankets and rags. The three huddle on both sides of me.

John hands me a blanket. "We hate that they are buying and selling people, but we are not going to let them start sending girls to work down here with a bunch of men. That's crazy."

Ned nods. "They've gone too far. We may have to speed up the take over."

"Take over?" I pull the blanket up to my chin.

"Lee, don't worry about it. We'll make sure that you are taken care of. I hate to think what would have happened..." He stops and drops his head in his hands.

"What?" I am so confused. These men need to fill me in on what they mean.

John shakes his head and leans on his back looking up at the ceiling. He rolls toward me and whispers. "They sent a girl down here before. A Merc got a hold of her. He was a mean one. He was mad that she couldn't keep up with the work and he beat her badly. She died before morning."

Ned nods. "We have to get her out before tomorrow night. Send out the message. We have one for extraction."

Sam, the quiet one, finally speaks, "My daughter was killed by a Merc. I'm not going to let that happen to someone else's daughter. I'll send the message to Lieutenant Thai." Sam pats my head. "I will die before I let anything happen to you."

"I don't want you to die." I had not known these men for long, but I already knew for sure that they were good people. They deserved better than to be owned people. Why is the whole world under the control of the Mercs? That *had* to change. If I escape, I will come back and save them. I have to. To traffic humans is wrong! It's just wrong! "If I make it, I'll come back for all of you."

The men smile at each other. Sam says, "That's sweet, but let's plan on getting you out first."

He's right. I can't save anyone until I'm free. I pull out my bullet four-leaf clover. Riley told me he wanted to make something lucky and good out of an object used for meanness and violence. That's what I like about Riley, always positive. I miss him. I roll the metal clover around in my hand. The thought of him soothes me. Somehow, I don't feel so alone now.

The next morning, Ned wakes me. "Time to get up. Be ready to move."

Sam explains, "When we get our breakfast, the three of us will create a diversion. When you see the guards and everyone distracted, run behind the serving table. I will point out the man who will help you as we go through the line." He hugs me. "Good luck, little one."

I nod. As we walk through the breakfast line, Sam points

to a boy serving eggs and grits paste. He's not much older than I am. The boy nods as he slops the goop onto my plate. It smells awful. I hope I don't have to eat it.

Servants do not eat well. They deliver food, but do not get to partake of the good portions. The owned ones eat what is left. On the farm, I always had enough to eat. We grew our own food. After that, I was given food as a Sponsored Companion, and then Baako delivered our food. I have never really been hungry or know what it is like to go without food. I never realized just how awful the owned servants were treated. Starvation! No wonder the workers have a hard time and struggle so much. They are malnourished.

Before I consume one bite, Sam, Ned, and John start to argue. It doesn't take long before our table and the rest of the tables join in. They are yelling about the lack of food. The guards come over. I slide under the table during the ruckus and make my way to the serving counter.

"Stay there for a moment." The boy dipping the egg paste slides a gigantic empty pot my way. "Climb in." I hesitate for a moment and he insists, "Now or never, girlie." He points to the melee. "You can stay and take your chances."

I glance over and see the guard slugging a few of the combatants. He's right; I have to trust him. I climb into the pot. It still has remnants of egg paste from this morning. It stinks like vomit, mold, and skunk all rolled into one. I pull out my metal clover from Riley. I hold it, concentrating on how it feels in my hand to take my focus away from the stench. The boy shuts the top. He might be saving me and I don't even know his name. What a strange world we live in. He seals the top and I hear him yell, "This one's ready. Load it on the truck."

I feel my container being shoved. I'm worried because I've only been locked in here a couple of minutes, but I'm already struggling to catch my breath. I shut my eyes and shallow my breathing to compensate. This might be a brief trip. I hold my breath as the container is twirled and then plopped hard on the ground.

Another voice yells, "Need help with this one, it's heavy." A different voice yells, "It's heavy because they didn't want to eat this slop." The first voice says, "It *is* nasty stuff." Laughter follows the comment. I feel myself lifted and slid onto a flat surface, which I assume, is a truck bed. It is hard to catch my breath.

I hear the boy's voice. "I need to check this one." The airtight buckles unclamp allowing air to make its way in. "Good to go!" He yells, and then whispers, "Good luck, girlie." Thank goodness some air! That would have been a short deadly jaunt. It's a few more minutes before I have the sensation of moving. They might be taking me to prison, or worse. I clutch Riley's metal clover tightly in my hand. It might be a long ride. Better save up my energy for whatever awaits me.

Chapter 19

When the truck stops, I hear worker's voices and have the sensation of being lifted. After being slammed around a few times, my large potted prison comes to rest. The room is dark. Must be nighttime. The sliver of light that was getting through is now gone. I sit inside my container of confinement, waiting. I keep hoping that I have a future. Unfortunately, the stench worsens when I wet myself. A girl can hold it just so long. I haven't eaten enough to warrant a need for the other. That would be bad. I'm starving, but it will be better if I wait to eat. Too bad my backpack full of food didn't make the trip with me. I hear rumblings about a journey to another camp after a few hours pass. No idea about the plans for my container.

Obviously, the people in this area are the poorest and have no say about their plight. I can tell by their talk. Conversations about the way the people are being treated run the gamut of livid to benign. I sit quietly, waiting to hear what happens next. Out of all the voices, I haven't heard one female voice and that concerns me. I am supposed to have escaped from an all-male internment to an underground escape of some sort. I have lost track of time although I think two days have passed. I am weak. I'm dehydrated because I don't even have enough in me to wet myself anymore.

Thoughts about Colt and Riley seep into my consciousness. Did my leaving cause them any problems? I steer my mind to focus on the answer to that question or any thought rather than the fact that I'm starving. It's a fleeting lapse at best before my attention reverts to my empty stomach. Fortunately, the egg paste I manage to scrape off the sides has a liquid base and that gives me a small amount of liquid in my system. I'm in trouble, big trouble. I'm going to die in here unless something changes. Soon.

Darkness falls again. I have to attempt to get out of this prison and save myself. It's quiet. I have no idea what I'll be escaping to, but I have to try. The lock is held by one catch of the buckle. I jimmy each latch back and forth until it releases completely. I slide the lid up. I slam my body from side to side until the pot topples. I'm weak and cramped. I crawl out of the pot onto the floor. It's takes a few moments for me to stretch out my legs. I rub them to help the circulation before I pull myself to a standing position and limp a few steps. I'm weary, but steady.

I'm in some sort of a storage closet. Shelves on each side are lined with large cans of beans, vegetables, and condiments. I spy a plastic bag half-opened of apples, grab one, and wolf it down. I eat the whole thing, core, and all. I find a pear and do the same thing. For the next few minutes, I sit on the floor and gorge myself on any food available. A couple of jugs of water rest on the floor and I turn one up, gulping so much that I start coughing. I stop, fearing that I will be heard. After a few moments, I realize no one is here but me so I eat more. I stand up again gingerly, taking baby steps until I can manage a full gait, trying to get my energy back.

I pull the four-leaf clover from around my neck and squeeze it for luck before stuffing it into my pocket. I relieve myself using the container the apples came in and then tie up the sack. After a few more minutes, I start to feel better. I straighten up everything. No way for me to hide the fact that I ate apples and pears and drank the water. I find another carrier to gather the plastic and my other garbage. My only hope is that whoever comes in this area won't remember what was here. There is so much food it would probably be next to impossible to keep a tally. I can't leave any trace. I set the container I was housed in upright and realign the top of the large pot as best I can. I gather the bag of my trash and crack the door to peek out. Black darkness paints my surroundings so I creep out, feeling my way around what seems to be a large storage barn. I deposit my sack of waste in what I hope is a garbage bin. After knocking my way down a couple of corridors, I spy a glimmer of light shining in a window. The small ray of moon light is just enough for me to locate the front door.

Outside, I see nothing but large storage units. No people, good or bad. I am just about to make a break for the woodsy area at the far end of the farm of storage sheds when I hear something.

It's a voice I don't recognize, but it's female. "I can't believe that we just got word about a stowaway from Ned. How long as she been here?"

A male voice answers, "Three days."

"Which shed?" The female asks.

The male answers, "I'm not sure. The note was lost for two days. We just got it."

"She might be dead. Did we get her name?"

The male answers again, "No. The only description we have is that she is wearing a mouse cap."

The woman stops. "She's dead. I just know it."

I have to take the chance. I walk out with my hands up. "It's me. I couldn't wait any longer. I was afraid I was going to starve to death."

He trains a gun on me. "Who are you?"

I pull off the mouse cap and my hair falls out. "Paisley. Ned, Sam, and John said that you could hide me."

The woman pushes his gun down. "We can."

I start to walk to them, but my feet give way and the whole world goes black.

"Paisley." Somebody shakes me. "Paisley, wake up.

You're safe now." It was the female voice from the storage-shed area.

I rest on a soft blanket. Warmth surrounds me. I feel for my clothes. I have on a different shirt and pants. I smell a whole lot better. I pat my clothes and around my neck, nothing. "Where's my clover?"

"I'm Via." She lifts my head for me to drink a glass of water. "I tossed your clothes out. I didn't see a clover."

"It was in the pocket of my pants." I sit up and my head spins. "It's important." I drop my head in my hands. "I need it."

"I'll see if I can find it. I know where your clothes are if they haven't been destroyed. I'll be back in a few minutes and let you know what I find." She leaves.

I scan the area. It's dark, but I can see a table and blankets strewn around with people sleeping on them. A couple of maps hang on one wall. They are covered with colored pins and notes. I can't make out what is written on them. In a few minutes, she returns with my dirty slacks. I sift through the pockets.

I sigh, "It's here." I pull the clover out and roll it in my hand before slipping its cord around my neck. It knocks against my chest. "Thanks." I say, "It's from—"

"No need to explain. We all have or want things to remember those that are important to us. Happy you found it." She smiles and pushes my hair back behind my ears. "Glad that Ned and Sam sent you here too."

I look around. "Where's here?"

"Sorry." She stands up and reaches for my hand. "Can you stand?"

"Yes." I come to my feet and steady myself. She holds my arm. I pull at her collar to gain my balance. Above her collar is a red birthmark in an unusual shape, a heart. I have never seen anything like it, yet it seems familiar. We are the same height. She is older, but there is something about her that puts me at ease. Her kind eyes. Her soothing way. It's hard to explain why I feel immediately comfortable with her.

"Via, is that your name?" She nods and I ask again, "Where is here?"

"Underground America." She walks me over to a crate and helps me to sit. "I'll try to explain."

A young boy who looks to be no more than thirteen brings a paper to Via. "Captain, we've found a ship. Our sources say that it is indeed from Germany." She signs the paper and the boy leaves.

I look at Via. "Did he call you Captain? Are you in charge?"

She smiles. "Yes. Women can be in charge too. Although you wouldn't know it from the way the world is now."

I nod. "Definitely." I can't figure out why I trust her, but I do. "So what do you do here and what's your interest in a ship from Germany?"

"Right to the point." She thumps me playfully on the back. "I like that. Maybe one day you'll be Captain and I'll retire."

"I don't understand why we need captains or colonels or lieutenants or anything." I jut out my chin.

"That's what Underground America is all about. We're trying to make a world where there's no need for the military ranks. No human trafficking, no owning of people." She sits on a crate beside mine and sighs. "But especially, we want to make sure there are no more viruses." She cocks her head. "Now I've answered some of your questions. It's your turn. Where are you from?"

"Germany. As a matter of fact, I escaped off that ship that the boy just told you about." No use lying now. I have to get help if I am going to get back to my family.

Her posture straightens. "You're not a spy, are you?"

"No!" I hop off the crate with hands on my hips and glare at her. "Of course not! I want the same as you. No one should be owned by someone else! I was an owned at one time. I served as a living doll."

She pulls me back down on the crate. "I didn't mean to upset you. You never know whom you can trust. We are just starting to make headway." She looks away for a minute then turns back. "Were you a Sponsored Companion?"

I nod.

"I heard about that. You serve as a doll for the wealthy children to play with."

I nod again. "It wasn't that bad. The princess was sweet."

She jumps up and holds both of my shoulders. "You know the royal family?"

"I used to. They tried to have me killed."

Her shocked expression unsettles me, but I continue, "In all fairness, it was the king who wanted me killed. The princess didn't have anything to do with it. She is innocent as is her father, the ambassador. He tried to save me and he did for a while until...never mind, that's a long story."

Her face softens. "You think the ambassador is a good man?"

"The best."

"I've heard that." Her softened features harden and she flusters for a minute looking from side to side. Then she suddenly stands erect and pulls me up. "Let me give you a tour of our facility."

For the next half an hour, she walks me through their command center. "Where we are now is a first station of an extensive underground secret society of supporters who work to end human trafficking and free others owned by the rich."

"Like the underground railroad?" I ask.

"I see you know some of America's history." She explains that they have been underground for quite a while, first taking refuge in the facility that used to house the staff at a deserted theme park. In that underground facility they were able to cook food using the kitchen and house a great many people. "At first, we only brought in those attempting to escape the virus."

"How did you know it wouldn't spread?" I pick up a couple of books on a table. I recognize one, *The Wizard of Oz*. "I know this book."

She takes it from my hand and returns it to the table. "It's a classic. If you were going to stay here, I'd let you keep it."

"Am I going somewhere else?"

"You're being transferred in a few minutes to the next

station, the facility in Orlando." She walks me to a door.

I stop just shy of the door. "You never told me how you didn't know the virus wouldn't spread to the underground."

"I wasn't here then. Unfortunately, it did spread. There were lots of deaths, but some survived."

I stare at her. "You were one of the survivors?"

She sighs. "No, I was the doctor relocated here after I was evacuated from my post. I was brought here to figure out why."

"And did you?" I ask.

"Still working on it." She opens the door. "Don't worry. Everyone who was infected died a long time ago. It's safe. Time for you to go."

A couple of young men clad in medical scrubs stand on the other side of the door. A jeep is behind them.

She hugs me. "These doctors will take you to a safe place. Good luck, Paisley."

"Will I see you again?"

She smiles and squeezes me again. "Most likely, no." She lets go and pushes me back, still holding onto my shoulders. "With our world as it is, I find that the truth is always the best. I could lie to you and tell you that I will be checking on you from time to time, but I have no way of knowing that. My place is here, coordinating the resistance and trying to find a way to support the ambassador."

I let out a long breath. "There is something that you might want to know."

"What?"

I purse my lips. I hate to give bad news. "Just before I escaped the ship, the ambassador was arrested and taken away. I saw him being driven off in a car."

She smiles. "Thanks for your honesty. We *did* know that and that's why I cannot go with you. We are in pursuit of that car. We're attempting to free the ambassador. If you'll excuse me, I'd better get back to my job. Take care."

I hug her one last time. "Save him. The ambassador is a good man and very important to me."

"He is important to us all." She closes the door.

I am placed in the back seat of the jeep and wrapped in a sheet. One of the men hooks an oxygen tube around my nose. Another rolls gauze around my head and body. He explains, "We are transporting you through the streets as a medical emergency. You have to look the part."

In a few minutes, I am gauzed up to not only disguise my identity, but to look like I am knocking on death's door.

As we ride through the streets of America, I see that the Mercs are not only policing Germany and Europe; they have a definite presence in America too. It's scary how much power the Mercs have. We are stopped three times. Once for an overturned car that has to be moved out of the way. The other two times for the Mercs to examine the bogus papers about me. I wonder what the papers say. I figure it says that I am contagious because after reading the document, the Mercs back up a little. The two men driving me are wearing protective masks.

It is almost dark. They speed up. The driver says, "We have to make it before curfew."

The other man points to a group of Mercs. "We only have a few minutes. We have to be off this road before curfew. Don't want them to look too closely at our patient."

The driver veers onto a deserted road. "Can't believe they would, with the patient listed as having early virus symptoms, but we can't be too careful."

That answers that question, no wonder not one of the guards or security personnel wants to get near me. The confinement of the gauze makes it impossible for me to move very much. I can only see out the front window of the vehicle and I can only observe what sits up high. I hope our journey is almost at its end.

After a few more turns into alleyways, we enter a long street. The driver says, "It's not too much farther."

I peek through the windshield and cannot believe what I catch sight of, sitting majestically, in front of me. It can't be. It's a miracle.

A big piece of heaven.

Chapter 20

Right in front of me, regally overlooking my little part of the world, is the castle from the postcard my mother keeps in a treasure box.

I murmur, "Orlando, where dreams come true."

The driver pulls up to an alcove. "Yeah, this is Orlando. Have you been to the castle or the park before?"

I shake my head. "Not really. I saw a picture of it once."

The other man gets out of the jeep. He unbuckles me; we both unroll my gauze to release my bondage. When I'm free, he says, "We need to hide the jeep. Grab the other side of the tarp."

In the corner sits a large piece of dark cloth. We pull it over the jeep to camouflage it.

"Covered," The driver says. "Follow me."

In a few minutes, the men duck **behind a hedge and descend into a concealed walkway.** I trail behind the men down a short flight of stairs and through a hidden door. Behind the door is a corridor. More steps. **As we go through an entrance at the end of the hallway, the walkways become illuminated by lanterns and widen into a large room.**

"Is there electricity down here?" I ask.

One of the men answers, "This area has its own power

source. Don't worry. You're safe here."

We come to a dining area full of tables and chairs and one of the men points to a chair. "Sit, while we find out where we're supposed to take you."

They leave. I watch the scene unfold around me. Men, women, and children scurry about. Some of the children carry food; some of the people haul lumber. Others hammer and nail wood in the midst of completing or starting some sort of construction. Old and young alike engage in various housekeeping duties such as folding clothes. Everyone is busy and smiling. I haven't seen this many happy people together in a long time, maybe never. Some are humming, some are singing. They seem content.

In the middle of the chaotic world and looming virus, I've hit a pocket where everyone is full of joy. Why are they so cheerful? Is it because they are free and safe? Children yell, "Mom! Dad!" Families are together. Smiling men and women, even some disabled people walking with crutches, work at various chores. A few have burn scars and some are disfigured. Is this a refuge for Uncounted and Undesirables?

I smile. For the first time in days, I have a little spot of happiness in my soul.

A man runs up, out of breath. He whispers to me, "Have you heard? It's the worst news ever. How will we ever overcome it?" His face is pale and his mood dire.

My cheerful mood disappears.

He trots off and encounters others. He speaks to them. Their expressions mirror the horror of the news. Smiles disappear. Workers, so happy and carefree just moments ago, turn ashen, their features consumed with fear.

A woman cradles a young girl and rocks her back and forth. She sits at the table beside me. "It's okay. It'll be okay. Don't worry. We will figure this out."

I lean over and ask, "Why is everyone so upset?"

"It's just a rumor." The woman rocks the child more. "It may not be true."

"What may not be true?" I ask.

"The ambassador has been killed."

The world twirls and I feel sick. My father is dead. How can that be? "It can't be true." I drop my head to the table. I cry.

The woman pats my hand trying to comfort me. "It's just a rumor. It'll be okay."

I glance up for a minute. This joyful world has just been covered with a dark fog, one that will suck goodness out of all of us. She is wrong. It will *not* be okay. How can anything ever be okay if my father is dead? And more than that, what will happen to the world if the only hope to end human trafficking and foster democracy has vanished? My father held the key to all of that. Nothing will be fine. It will never be the same. All hope is lost. I let go, crying with the masses.

For the rest of the day, people sport bloodshot eyes as the sobbing continues. I am taken to a holding area without much instruction except to bunk here and wait for directions later. Everything is falling apart, I need to get out of here and make it back to the ship with my family, Riley, and Colt. I have no idea how to go about accomplishing that.

That night, I sit on my bunk, numb. Those around me are distraught and without direction. I am right there with them. The happiness that permeated this underground city is now gone. My head falls in my hands as I am hit with the realization that my father, my real father, is dead. It is too much to bear. I cry myself to sleep.

I wake up sadder than I have ever been. I have a hard time moving. I don't have to change clothes because I slept in them. I see a rumpled person when I look in the mirror. I feel on the inside how I look on the outside, discombobulated and without purpose.

"They're serving breakfast now," says a girl on the bunk next to me. "I'm supposed to take you."

"Not hungry."

"I know," she replies. "Me neither, but they didn't give us a choice."

I throw the blanket on the worn cot where I had slumbered the night before and shuffle into the next room. A long table is set up and people are getting their breakfast. Breakfast consists of fresh citrus, oranges and grapefruits, as well as some sort of oatmeal mixture. It's probably good, but I can't taste it. My taste buds must be in shock like the rest of me. I go through the motion of eating. I'm overwhelmed by the news, and the bigness of it all. I feel much older than my fifteen years.

The morning drags, then it is time for another tasteless meal. Groups sit at the tables for lunch.

One girl with red hair asks, "What are we going to do now that the ambassador is dead? How can we expect a win for democracy? We have to free everyone, all of the owned and disenfranchised people of the world."

A dark-skinned young man stomps into the room muttering to himself. He then slams his plate on the table and food flies everywhere. "We can't just give up and we aren't indentured servants. Indentured servants have the chance of being freed. We are *slaves*. When the wealthy own us, there is nothing we can do to free ourselves. That is the difference."

I am reminded of my farm and the army of children training to fight and die if they have to for the cause of freedom. If they didn't give up, then I shouldn't either. There has to be hope. Just has to be. I need to find it. We all need to find it. Now.

I scoot over to the girl with red hair. "There's always hope. *Everyone* is scared. It's okay to be scared. I'm scared too." I squeeze her arm. "What's your name?"

"Julia." She ekes out.

I take in a deep breath. "Julia, we will figure a way out of this. Sometimes when a celebrated leader dies, it makes the cause become greater. Ever heard of martyrs?" She shakes her head meekly and I continue, "I've read about them in books so I can tell you about them. Joan of Arc was a martyr. After her death the cause moved forward using her death to spark their rebellion." I can't believe that I am so calmly able to talk about this. Am I dead inside? How can my father's death mean so little to me? Somehow as I am saying this to her, it makes me feel better. How strange. I continue, "Maybe that will happen here and someone will take the ambassador's place."

The dark-skinned young man sits down beside me. "Like who, you?" He rubs his chin. "Aren't you new? How do we know you're not a spy?" He glares at me. "You might be in with the people who killed the ambassador. We have no way of knowing. Maybe you've been sent here to—I don't know—to discover our secrets."

Julia slams her hand down. "Listen to yourself Eddie. You're not making any sense."

"She's right, you're not making any sense." I hoarsely whisper under my breath. "If you only knew how far off you really are." I stare at Eddie. He's old enough to know better. He should be calming the young ones down, not riling them up. I'm indignant. "I'm not here to spy. I *want* to leave. I need to get back to the ship that docked here a few days ago. I have to try to save my family and friends."

"That ship?" Eddie shakes his head. "Haven't you heard that it's leaving tomorrow? There's no way that you can get back on that ship."

I jump up and put my hands on my hips. "I might not be able to get on *that* ship, but I have to try. And if I don't make it, then I have to find another way to Europe. I *have* to save my family." I slam my fists in the air. "I just have to." I look at them. "I refuse to give up." I take in a deep breath and point my finger first at Julia and then at Eddie. "You, you two! I'm talking to you! Help me figure this out. Any ideas? I am not just going to let this happen to our world." I bang my fists on the table. "You, all of you, should be standing up for what's right too." I point a finger inches from his face.

Julia stands up beside me. "She's right. We need to do something instead of just sitting around crying all day."

A few more stand. In a few minutes, the entire group of adults and children has risen. Eddie lifts me on top of the table. "Do it then. Rally the troops. You're in charge."

This is not what I wanted. I have no idea what to say or how to say it. I rub the bullet clover corded around my neck. What would Riley do? Or Colt? How can I let my father's death be in vain? I can only tell them what I know to be true. I say, "I can tell you stories about what I've seen. I can tell you what I know."

The resistance group contently listens as I regale them of the stories of our farms, farm life, the hidden caves, and the harvest. I also enlighten them about how the Mercs stole the farms from us, the rightful owners, and how the newspapers reported it wrong.

I share more stories about Colt and my escape. About the ship, the princess, the ambassador, the threats, and many failed attempts on the ambassador's life. How through all of this adversity, the ambassador always wanted to forge ahead for democracy.

I enlighten them about my family, the Sponsored Companions Program, the Uncounteds, and the Undesirables. I tell them about the Mercs, their blood lust, and how they kill people for no reason. How Colt and I were to be killed and how the ambassador spared us.

I tantalize them with the luck and the Merc's surprise announcement about our escape back to my farm. I share about the resistance that we encountered and the army of children we were training. I tell them how I came over on the ship and how I came to be here. The longer I talk, the more people gather into the food area. By the time I stop talking, the area is packed.

I pull Julia up on the table beside me. "Tell them your story."

Julia tells about how she was stolen from her family. She wandered the streets until Captain Via took her in. Next, Eddie tells his tale. One by one, each of the group stands and gives an account of how they have been persecuted since the virus outbreak.

A few elderly people paint the picture of what life was like before the virus. They discuss what a democracy is and how everyone in the world cooperates with each other. Americans explain their former political party organizations and an elderly woman from Europe educates us about her country's leadership structure.

Discussions continue for so long that it is time for another meal. As the group sits down to eat, strategies to bring the world together are thrashed out. This talk makes me feel so much better. Nothing could pierce the agony of the loss I feel about my father, but planning some positive actions makes me hopeful that there still might be a chance to defeat the king and the Mercs. The one thing everyone agrees with is that this world *is* worth winning and that our lives, all of our lives, flawed or perfect, are worth saving.

Eddie takes a swig of water. "I can get you on a boat back to Germany."

I drop a fork full of food back to my plate. "You can get me on the ship?"

"No, not that one." He leans in to whisper. "There is a ship that I know of that is leaving soon for Germany transporting a very important person."

"Who?" I ask.

"I'm not sure, but someone who is in danger here. They're trying to hide him." Eddie scoops some beans on his fork.

"Maybe the ambassador isn't really dead," I say.

"I wish." Eddie puts the fork back down on his plate. "But this was set up before your ship came in so it can't be him."

It was too much to ask for. My father is truly dead. My spirit sinks for a moment before I ask, "Why are they going to Germany?"

Eddie takes a bite and chews. "There's a resistance group in Germany."

"I wonder if it is with the same group I was telling you about?"

"This one calls itself PACO."

I shake my head. "Never heard of them, but we need the resistance groups to join together, don't you think?"

"Definitely." He picks up his tray. "Come with me. Let's see when the group is leaving and if we can get you on their ship."

"There is not any *if* to it. I *have* to be on that ship. It's my only hope." I follow him with my tray. We scrape them and give them to the kitchen staff. "Is it a big boat?"

"Big enough." He laughs. "You don't know, do you?"

"Know what?" I ask.

"It's a pirate ship."

Chapter 21

Eddie leads me into another area, full of tables and chairs. He pulls a chair from the stack, points to it, and I sit. He grabs another for himself and sits facing me.

He says, "Groups of resistance fighters from the states, Europe, Asia, the outer islands, and Australia had been trading for about three years when we discovered each other."

I ask, "I don't understand why it's called a pirate ship."

He laughs. "That's the best part. Back when everyone was under quarantine, I escaped on a ship with a group of my friends and family. For a long time, we waited out in the ocean."

I scrunched up my face. "Why?"

"Because if we're out on the ocean and no one is sick then how can diseases find you. Right?"

I nod. It did sound like a foolproof plan. What better quarantine than millions of miles of ocean?

"Anyway while we were out to sea a ship came by so we started talking to them. They told us of other ships. It started with four ships roped together out in the middle of the Atlantic Ocean. We became experienced fishermen and caught rainwater to drink. It was idyllic. We had small boats so we could travel from ship to ship."

"Why did you ever come to shore?" I ask.

"Lots of reasons. We started running out of supplies. We wanted to know what happened with the rest of the world. Plus, our palates were aching for something more than fish. The quarters were so cramped, we began to go stir crazy."

"I understand, but it was very risky coming back to shore." I shake my head. He picks up a packet and nods toward me. I ask, "What is it?"

He unwraps the packet. "Chocolate. You should try it. It's hard to come by. It's more of a luxury. I only get it when someone raids a stockpile somewhere. I remember loving it when I was young. Before the virus."

"I might try a bite." I put the brown substance on my tongue. The sensation of flavor is unbelievable as it melts in my mouth. I wait until the last morsel is gone. "Oh my goodness, this is the best tasting stuff. I can see why it's a luxury. I'm surprised there is any left. But you still haven't answered my question. Why did you ever come back to shore?"

"We ran out of staples: sugar, rice and that sort of thing. In addition, we had a baby born on board and needed different kinds of food. The mother was able to nurse, but we couldn't feed the baby properly. At first, we would send a small boat. We floated the big ship miles from shore then a few of us would travel out. During these excursions, we realized what had happened with our world."

I lean in. "What do you mean?"

He licks his fingers. "It was sad. When we escaped in our ships five years before, our world was a communication empire. We could buy whatever we wanted and the world was at peace. Of course, when we left there was also a virus ravaging everyone. I wasn't sure that anyone had survived. But I wasn't prepared for what I found when I did finally get here." He takes another small piece of the chocolate and hands the rest of the package to me.

I pinch off another piece and place it on my tongue, not talking until it is gone. "What did you find?"

"It's good isn't it?" He smacks his lips for a moment then focuses back on me. "Where was I? Oh, yeah. When we returned, the world was being controlled by the Mercs."

"I know. The Mercs controlled our farms, stole our harvest and then a few months ago, took us out of the picture entirely."

"Same story all over. Same story, different places." He takes the paper from my hand and licks it for the leftover chocolate. "The Mercs re-commissioned the communications devices left by the military when they abandoned their posts after the virus outbreak. For the past year or so, they have been using them to coordinate this take-over."

"Is that when you decided to join the resistance?" I ask.

"Yes. At first, we just bartered for grains and staples. We were happy to just keep it like that. We would stay on the open sea and trade fish for our needs, but then—"

"Something happened to change your mind," I interject.

"Yeah, isn't that how it always happens?"

"What?" I ask.

"We found people in the open waters, floating on a single piece of wood, most likely a left over part of the hull of a ship. Some shared their horrible stories. It seems that a ship had thrown what they considered undesirable people and what they called Uncounteds overboard. Although there were a few dead, most had survived days on that piece of drift wood."

"How old were you when the virus hit?"

"Fifteen."

I smile. "That's how old I am now."

"Hope your next fifteen years are better than this fifteen."

"Me too. What happened to the survivors?"

"They were definitely survivors. They amazed me." He shifts a little in his chair. "They had survived for days with no food. Some were so sick they could hardly walk, but they survived. They flagged us down and we took them in. After hearing their stories, our ships would troll the waters searching for stray people who had been cast overboard. That's how we built up our numbers."

"Are there lots of you?" I ask.

"Yes. Our numbers are many. Our people resist being owned, bought, and sold. They fight against the Mercs and royal's control of the world. We coordinate with every continent. Underground movements exist everywhere, waiting on for the right time to declare ourselves."

I ask, "When do you plan to do that?"

"We thought we wouldn't have to. We thought our fight was about to be over since the ambassador was supposed to make the world a democracy again and the virus was eradicated. But now—"

I choke back a sob. "The ambassador's death has changed all of that."

He nods. "Yes. It is a great blow. We are sending a ship over to Germany to try to make a new plan. That's the ship I need to get you on if you hope to see your family again."

I drop my head. "My family is on a ship too. The "Queen Nalani". I will probably never see them again."

He squeezes my shoulder. "Never give up hope. As long as your family is still alive. As long as we are all alive, there is still hope. Weren't you the one who just gave that speech about hope and never giving up?"

I smile weakly. "I guess."

"*I guess* is not good enough. I'm going to have to move quickly if I want to get you on that ship. I'm risking my life for you. I will most likely have to travel with you, so if *I guess* is all you can muster to say then maybe—"

"I was not giving up hope of winning just getting on that ship." I straighten up. "You don't know me, Eddie, but I will fight until I am no longer breathing. If you think we can catch up with the ship, then count me in."

He stands. "That's what I was hoping to hear you say. No time to waste. We need to leave now."

"How?" I ask.

"Quietly and carefully."

We spend the next few minutes winding our way out of the underground and walk up flights of stairs until we come to a door. Dawn is breaking. For the first time, I look at my surroundings as we come into the brightness. There it stands: the castle from the postcard. It's certainly not as beautiful and picturesque as it obviously once was, but there it is just the same. I am let down – I'm not sure what I was expecting. That my dreams would come true if I found Orlando. That I would somehow come to this beautiful castle and all of my problems would disappear. That most certainly did not happen. Here I am on foreign soil with people I don't know, trusting them to carry me back across an ocean on a pirate ship.

I look around. "What was this place?"

"It used to be a very popular theme park," Eddie whispers as we walk to awaiting trucks. "People from all over the world came here to have fun. It was an escape from the humdrum of daily life."

"The humdrum of daily life, wouldn't we all like to get a taste of a boring life now. I don't know about you, but lately my life is a constant battle to stay alive."

He nods. "Mine too."

I see a few remnants of a Ferris wheel and roller coaster. I recognize them from the pictures that surrounded the castle picture on the postcard. What a wondrous place this must have been! Now look at it: rubble and rust. "Do you think we can ever make the world even close to what it used to be?"

"No, of course not." He guides me around a curve. "We will make it better. Then all of the future generations will marvel. The world will rise again and it will be a more loving place. That is, if I have anything to say about it."

I like this Eddie and his ideals. I can't believe how lucky I've been to escape from that work camp. My luck is continuing as I have now run into Eddie who knows about a pirate ship going back to Germany. It is as if I have a lucky charm. I reach for the four-leaf clover bullet and rub it. A tear runs down my cheek as I realize I now have the lucky charm. What if Riley needs the luck? He has to have been caught by now. What will they do to him? The thought of Riley and Colt and my family still on that ship makes me move a little faster.

He leads me to a clearing where trucks are being loaded for the next shipment to the vessels. "Our ships are not near the "Queen Nalani" liner. It is docked miles from there. We have to hurry. We are going on the truck part of the way, and then we have to ride bikes. You up for it?"

"I am."

We crawl into the front seat of the truck. The driver, a tall man with dark hair, says, "They don't check until we reach the dock. You two can climb out before then. I'll tell you when."

Eddie nods and we start on a very quiet trip. No words are exchanged. I scan the countryside. It's flat and devoid of vegetation. What made anyone want to live here? There are remnants of trees. It's not until we get close to the ports that I notice people. We stop and the driver lets us out. Eddie uncovers bicycles from the bed of the truck, pulls one out, points to another, motioning for me to retrieve it. I obey. We duck into the grove, for cover. The driver rides off.

The trek through the grove is bumpy, but nice. The fall weather is crisp, albeit humid. Bavarian air is so light with the altitude. The humidity makes me miss the autumn in Bavaria. I hope that I can find my way back there soon. We travel for a few miles before we come upon a highway. It's a two-lane road with cracked pavement. Probably the hot sun and no upkeep has lent to the wear and tear of this causeway. Even with the cracks in the road, it is an easier bike ride. We are able to coast on the downhill part. We walk alongside our bikes when the climb is steep.

We are riding beside a grove, when Eddie suddenly yells, "Stop! Hide!" He jumps off his bike and pulls it into one of the tree groves.

I follow concealing my bike, just before a large caravan of trucks races by. "Who are they?"

"That's the scout jeep." He points. "Must be some of the Mercs. Don't know why they are coming this way. We'll have to be careful and stay out of their way. We're not on this road much longer."

"Where are they heading?"

He crouches lower. "If I had to guess, it would be to your "Queen Nalani" ship."

"Why?"

"I don't know. Maybe they want more security since the ambassador was killed." He plucks a blade of grass and puts it in his mouth.

I clench the handles on the bicycle. "Why would they need more security? I think it's probably the king who had the ambassador killed?" I hold back a tear.

"Why would you think that?" He glances at me. "You know more than you told us, don't you?"

"Maybe I can tell you more later," I say with a nod. "The one thing I can tell you now is that I thought a lot of the ambassador."

"I can tell," he says, lowering his head. "I hear more trucks, they're close." He pushes the top of my head down. "You'll have to tell me later. We'll need to hurry once this convoy passes." He crouches lower and I follow doing the same. "Wait a minute."

The rest of the trucks pass slower. Perched high atop the middle truck is a man with a black beard and plumed hat. His uniform is adorned with a white satin coat with gold braiding. I assume the rest of his outfit is as costumed although I can't see it since he is seated.

"Who's that?" I ask.

"That's our problem." Eddie grimaces. "Emperor Richard the Great."

"I'm confused."

Eddie throws the blade of grass down. "You probably should be. He used to be just Richard something or another and now he has renamed himself Emperor Richard the Great. Don't know where he got those gaudy clothes. Probably out of a museum. Maybe something of Napoleon's for all I know."

"What does Richard the Great do?"

"He's the blood-thirsty head of the American Mercenaries. He came up with the idea for the identification tattoos and then the rules about limits of people living together. It is because of those limits that we have Uncounteds. All of that led to the human trafficking problems that we now have. He thinks nothing of stealing. His lust for control knows no bounds. He has wealth and power and is very corrupt."

Eddie stands his bike up. "It's clear. We can go now."

"Where did he get all of the wealth?" I ask.

"Probably the same place that they get the wealth in Germany. From the hard-working poor, by stealing their lands and harvest. But this Merc got a lot of his power from the king." He pedals back out into the street.

I follow him. "King Ahomana?"

He nods his head. "One and the same. Evil always finds evil." He pedals faster. "We need to hurry. They looked like they were searching for something or somebody. We don't want to get caught." He coasts for a minute. "Must be something or somebody really important to pull the emperor out of his hiding place. He is always in hiding."

I catch up with him. "Do you think they are planning something big?"

"I guess you could say that. A take-over. I think all of this is leading up to the king taking over the world. If that happens, then none of us are safe."

We turn off to another road and wind up and down through barren stretches of road. I have to admit, the trail is confusing. This group is serious about keeping their whereabouts hidden. It reminds me of the maze. Thinking about the maze makes me nostalgic for a minute. I have to find my way home, but more than that, we have to free our world.

"It's right up here," Eddie says. We coast around a long curved downward stretch of highway. When we reach the bottom of the hill, a ship with a large sail comes into view. It looks like a pirate ship or the pictures in a book of what I think a pirate ship should look like. A flag decorated with skull and crossbones adorns one of the masts. People are milling about and loading supplies. We ride up on the bicycles.

"We made it." Eddie smiles back at me and waves to a man in a sailor hat. "This is Paisley. She's going with you as far as Bavaria." Eddie tips his head at the man. "This is Captain Cox."

I reach out my hand while balancing on the bicycle. "Nice to meet you and thanks for letting me tag along."

Captain Cox shakes my hand and winks. "It's not a free ride. You'll have to work for your keep. You're not afraid of work are you?"

I grip his hand tightly. "Been a hard worker all my life."

"We'll start you in the kitchen." He points to our bicycles. "Let's get the bikes stored and Eddie can show you the way to the kitchen and to your quarters." He looks over at Eddie. "It's going to be a full ride this time. We really need you to come with us."

"Sure, if you need me." Eddie gets off his bike. "Expecting any trouble?"

The captain cocks his head toward the people gathered on the road beside the ship. "We have a high priority guest with us. If word leaks out he is onboard, we might be a target."

Eddie rolls his bike up and peers over to get a better look. "Any idea who?"

The captain motions for two workers to take the bikes. The men gather our rides and then the captain motions for us to follow him. "I'll introduce you." The captain pulls out a paper from his pocket. "But first, have you seen this nonsense and rhetoric they are spouting to the people now?" He unfolds the paper and hands it to Eddie.

Eddie stops and reads for a moment. "It says here that the resistance killed the ambassador." Eddie slaps the paper to his leg. "Nothing could be farther from the truth. We were trying to save him. To rescue him!"

The captain shakes his head. "I know that and you know that to be true, but people will read this and believe it. How can we fight this? They control the press."

Eddie folds the page and hands it back to the captain. "It's about time we start controlling the press, or at least get our hands dirty."

"Glad you think that way, old boy. It's wonderful to have you with us on this historic journey." The captain slaps Eddie on his back. "Because that is just what we plan to do and we have just the right genius to start our communication back up."

We walk toward the group. A boy who looks about my age or maybe a little younger than I am steps out. "Hello,

Captain. Thanks for having me."

The captain shakes the boy's hand. "Of course, we plan on using all of that technical knowledge. None of us has had the access you have had. We could not have hoped for a better inside man. I have recruited a helper for you. This is Eddie. He used to work with short wave radios and that sort of thing. Thought you could use him. He brought along this girl. If you want, she could work with you too. I was going to have her go to the kitchen, but she could fetch things for you."

The boy scans me up and down. "You're right. We probably need someone to get our food and supplies."

My face flushes with extreme anger so much so that I think I'm going to faint. I clench my fists so hard that my fingernails bring blood to the inside of my hands. I am enraged that they think I am so useless, but I bite my tongue. I'll prove my worth to them. I take in a deep breath to calm my voice. "Since when do you think girls cannot do anything? I'll have you know—"

The captain grabs me around the waist, pulling me away. "Sorry, I guess the kitchen will be a better choice."

The boy grins. "No, she'll do. The last thing I need around me is someone who caters to my every want and need. I've had that way too long. It's time I started going out on my own and use what I've learned to carry on my father's legacy. God rest his soul." With that last statement, the boy bows his head and the others around the ship do too.

"Who was your father?" I ask.

"You don't know who my father was?" The boy gazes deep into my eyes.

I shake my head.

The boy takes in a deep breath. "Where have you been that you don't know who *I* am?"

Eddie bows. "We just picked her up off the "Queen Nalani." She was sold as a boy into the pits and the men there sent her to our underground. They didn't want her to get hurt. They can't protect a girl in their midst."

The boy nods. "They were probably right. Caged men do crazy things. Good call." He bows back to Eddie and looks at me. "What's your name?"

"Paisley."

"Paisley. I am Oliver. My father was the assassinated Ambassador Grayson." He reaches out to shake my hand, but I feel myself falling.

My brother. He's my brother!

Chapter 22

I see Oliver's face when I open my eyes. He is waving his hands over me and asks, "You okay?"

I sit up. "Sorry, I haven't eaten in a while. It probably caught up with me."

He pulls me up.

I'm touching my brother's hand. I must work with him. I have to get to know him. I gather my senses and explain, "Look, Oliver. I can help you. I'm smart. I'd like to work with you instead of the kitchen. Eddie is the only person I know on this ship."

He shakes my hand. I smile. I know exactly how old he is. Fourteen and I know that he is a genius with communications. I'm so glad that my father was able to share that with me before... I stop with that thought, fearing that I might tear up.

I want to get to know my brother especially since my father is dead. He is the last of my birth family. "I'd work hard and not be any trouble. I promise. You'd be doing me a favor. I'd appreciate it." I hold my breath.

"Sure." He grins. "But you may be in for more than you bargained for. Seems my disappearance has brought out the emperor. He's hot on my trail." He chuckles. "He wants to assassinate me. He's mad that I sabotaged the communications program I had previously set up for him and the king." He smiles a wry grin. "Of course, it could be because I stole vital communication instruments when I escaped so we could set up our own communications system. That loss will cripple his organization." His eyebrow lifts. "You might get caught in the crossfire."

"I'll take my chances."

The captain motions for his men to gather Oliver's belongings. "We have a place set up for you below. You can work and sleep there. There are three bunks, but it's all together." He looks over at me. "Hope you don't mind sleeping in the same room as these two."

"No problem." I pick up one of Oliver's bags. "We're going to be working. I'm sure the sleeping will be just a side note."

Oliver slings the last bag over his shoulder. "We're going to get along fine. Where are you from, Paisley?"

"Bavaria." It slips out, before I can think. Then I question my hesitation, why can't I tell him where I'm from? He would never connect.

"My father used to talk of Bavaria. He and my mother were there before the virus and her death."

"How did she die?" Did he get the same story as me?

"She died after the virus. My sister, Penelope, died too."

I nod. Of course, I know this isn't true since I'm alive. So sad. I will never know the whole truth now since our father has been assassinated.

Eddie, Oliver, and I are led to a large cabin. Housed inside is the ship's main communication, archaic looking with tubes and wires. Can Oliver really make sense out of all of this?

He rushes to the microphones. "It's better than I thought. We have short wave capabilities as well as digital. I can get both kinds of communication. From this ship, we should be able to communicate with the entire PACO society."

I throw my bag down on the floor. "You've heard of the PACO resistance all the way over here?"

He pulls a wire and hooks it to another wire. "How do

you think we found out about the resistance? I've been secretly communicating with them for months."

I pull books off a chair and sit down. "Before the ambassador and his wife made it to Germany."

"Back then they didn't have so much organization. They didn't even have a name. The PACO title just started about a month ago."

"What does PACO mean?" I ask.

Oliver lines up wires. "I have no idea. All I know is that when they started calling themselves PACO, they seemed more focused."

"See what I'm doing here?" He places the wires on the desk according to their color. "This is what I need you to do first."

For the next two hours Oliver, Eddie, and I work on dismantling the old communications system. Oliver takes the microphone apart and blows on each of the parts. He asks Eddie to bring him a component from one of his bags. Oliver takes that piece and places it in the microphone.

He clicks it to the "on" position. "This works. Do you hear the hum?" A grin fills his face. "Now on to the motherboard."

Eddie claps his hands. "Well done. Let's take a quick break. We're going to be shoving off soon. Let's go up on deck and watch, and then we can get something to eat. Maybe even some sleep after that."

I nod. "Sleep might make me more alert."

Oliver holds the microphone for a second then places it back down. "Guess we do need to eat. Besides, we're going to be on the open sea for a while. Plenty of time to finish the work. No telling who we might contact." His eyes twinkle as he talks.

My brother really does seem to know a lot about electronics. I haven't seen anyone this excited about anything since I saw Gretel working with the ambassador. Fear shoots through me. If Gretel was the ambassador's right-hand person then what will become of her now that the ambassador is gone? What about Mom, Colt, or Riley? I need to focus. It will be good to help my brother with his project, but my ultimate goal has to be to save my family still captive on the ship. Riley is in this spot because of me. I rub the lucky charm around my neck. I wish I could give this luck to all of them.

I sigh, releasing my thoughts when I arrive on the deck with Eddie and Oliver. Ropes are hoisted and the ship readies for its voyage. It's getting dark. Sun will set soon.

"Do they put on any lights?" I ask as the darkness of the night sets in.

Eddie waves his arms around. "It's the open sea. No lights should be out here unless they are a ship connected to the king. If we put on lights, then we might be discovered."

I widen my eyes. "How will we know where to go?"

"Instruments." He grins back at me. "You don't know anything about ships, do you?"

I crook my head. "I'm a farm girl. Where would I learn about ships?"

He nods. "The king travels in a set path. All we have to do is to avoid that route once we get out to sea. But getting out to sea, we are still visible. **We don't want a person walking the beach to see us and report us.** Do we?"

I shake my head. "There are people free enough to walk on the beach?"

Oliver laughs. "He just told you about the possibly of getting caught, and all you can think of is how people can walk on the beach?"

"When you've been forced to stay in one place all of your life, it's hard to imagine what it would be like to wake up one day and decide to take a walk. I've had orders to stay on the farm all of my life. Then I escaped to the "Queen Nalani" where I became a Sponsored Companion. Then, I followed more orders."

"What's a Sponsored Companion?" Oliver leans on the rail.

It's hard to be so careful with what I say. I might accidentally clue him in on our real connection. I want him to know that he is my brother, but not just yet. "A Sponsored Companion does not have the freedom to decide to walk on the beach whenever they want. Basically, a Sponsored Companion is an owned person. To do the bidding of those who own them. I was a SC, but I escaped and now I'm here." I take a deep breath. That whole speech didn't make much sense to someone who hadn't lived through it, but maybe my indignation about it all will make him not ask any more questions.

"Sorry, I can tell it's a touchy subject." It worked, he's going to drop it. "If it makes you feel any better, I've been a prisoner my whole life too."

I slide beside him and grab the rail. "How could you have been a prisoner?" I ask. "You were the ambassador's son."

He gazes out onto the shoreline. "There are many different kinds of prisons."

I don't ask any more questions. Eddie finds a chair and we all watch the sun melt into the dark orange horizon. Funny, the sun seems the same no matter where I am in the world. Each day brings hope for something new. A new freedom. Finding my family. Breaking the communication code. Finding out more about my brother. Tomorrow could be the best day ever. I just have to have hope. I have to hold onto it. I'm free now in a sense. If there were a beach around, I could choose to walk on it. There is a certain amount of happiness in just knowing that.

Oliver spends three days redoing all of the wires and completely gutting the motherboard in order to reconstruct it. Being his assistant proves to be a learning experience for me and I enjoy finding out about the inner workings of his contraption. I am filled with great anticipation when he hooks the last wire and says, "We need to try to communicate."

Eddie says, "Should I get the captain?"

Oliver turns the microphone on and off. "Not just yet. Let's make sure that it works." He flicks the microphone on and holds the button down. "This is Ship 0204. Does anybody hear me?"

He repeats the question seven more times. I'm counting.

"Identify your allegiance." A booming voice rips through the speaker in the motherboard.

Oliver holds the button down. "PACO."

The voice asks, "Location?"

Oliver replies, "America, you?"

"Bavaria." The voice sounds again.

"That's where I'm from." I shout and jump up.

"Shush!" Oliver holds up his hand. "We don't know who this is." He pushes the button again. "Code?"

The speaker is silent for a couple of seconds. "I'll name the first part of the code you name the last. Agreed?"

"Agreed." Oliver speaks into the microphone. He presses the button once again. "CO."

The speaker immediately responds. "PA."

Oliver breathes a sigh of relief. "What's the status there?"

The speaker booms. "We are organizing an army. Consisting mostly of children. We number in the thousands. Our base of operation has not been infiltrated. We are joined by a family that has been most helpful."

Oliver presses the button again. "We are on our way to you. I'll bring you more information. The Americans and Europeans need to work together."

"I will send you the coordinates of our rendezvous point." A few beeps follow.

I ask, "Are those the coordinates?"

Oliver nods as he writes down the numbers. "We'll find it on the map." He presses the button again. "Over and out."

"Wait!" The voice booms again. "We need a password for when we meet."

I push the button on the microphone and offer. "What about you say, "Roses are red and violets are blue" and then he says the line, "If you say this line then I'll know it's you." Will that work?"

Laughter seeps out of the airways. "I can do that. Don't know who the girlie is, but she's a keeper."

Oliver presses the button. "Okay, we'll use that line. But about the girl, you might want to meet her before you say that."

I sock him in the arm.

"What is the name of your operation?" The voice booms

again. "What do I call you?"

"SONOL," Oliver says and I read what he has written on the paper "SON-OLIVER" with the last four letters marked out. SONOL, clever.

"One more question SONOL. There is an Aunt Sandra here in Bavaria who would like to know if you came across any young people named Colt, Paisley, or Riley. She's worried about them."

I grab the microphone and press the button. "This is Paisley. Tell Aunt Sandra that I am safe, but we will have to rescue Riley and Colt." I take my finger off the button for a second and then press it again. "What about the farm? Did she get the children from the farm?"

The voice booms. "She did. Some are still there, but all are safe." The speaker squawks one last time. "PACO over and out."

Oliver grabs the microphone and sets it down on the desk. "*You're* involved with the resistance."

I frown. "You didn't believe me?"

He sits back in his chair. "Not really. That was a crazy story you told. I thought you might be a spy."

I drag another chair over and take a seat. "If you thought that, then why did you let me work in here with you?"

He shrugs. "There's no escape for you here. I thought you might give us some information. I want to apologize for doubting you."

I smirk and nod. "Apology accepted." A satisfying tingle flows through me.

I could wallow in anger about how he did not believe me, but we have bigger issues. How are we ever going to get our power back when we don't know whom to trust? "We need a patch or tattoo or something that identifies us to each other, but doesn't give us away to the enemy."

Eddie nods. "That's a great idea." He pulls out some paper. "What do you have in mind?"

I think for a moment before an image pops into my mind. I draw the broken egg. "I saw this on a train and also tattooed on a resistance fighter in Bavaria."

"What does it mean?" Oliver asks.

"Below it was scrawled one word—freedom. I guess that's what it means. If we're trapped like yolks inside the egg, we can't do anything. We have to break the shell to be free."

Oliver pulls the paper with the drawing over to illuminate it under the light. "I like it. Let's get this started. We can use this drawing as a guide. Maybe we can make patches for people to put on their shirts or carry. This way we can identify ourselves to each other."

I point to the microphone. "Next time you contact them tell the Bavarian people to find Lieutenant Drake. He'll help them. Last time I saw him was when I was in Hamburg. He offered to help us then. He told us he was with the resistance and had connections to other underground cells."

"Of course I've heard of him," says Eddie, opening the door. "He's one of the leaders. Do you know everybody?"

I smile. "Not quite everybody, but maybe enough to get us started."

For the next four days, we communicate daily with the Bavarian resistance faction. Oliver tries to reach the Americans with no luck. Frustration sets in; we have to be able to connect the continents.

Fortunately, some of the women on board have experience with sewing and they fashion a broken egg patch that we are to carry with us at all times. It is constructed to unravel if we pull on one particular thread of the egg to protect our identity in case we are caught by the enemy. It is a masterful piece of work.

On the ninth day, the sea is rough. Oliver searches me out to inform me that a message has gotten through to the Americans.

"What's the name of the resistance leader in America?" I ask.

"Her name is—"

"Her?" I question.

Oliver laughs. "That's funny coming from you. I

remember on the very first day, you told me clearly that women were just as useful as men. You said that you shouldn't be put in the kitchen." He winks at me. "I thought you were speaking the truth, but then again I thought maybe you just didn't know how to cook." He chuckles again.

I feel my cheeks burning. "Of course. I just meant." I pause trying to think of something else to say. When nothing comes to mind, I mumble, "I'm just surprised that's all."

Oliver relishes my discomfort and obviously wants it to continue so he asks, "Okay smarty pants, since you know so much. Tell me the name of the woman leader for the Americans." He leans up against a wall in the room. "If you can name her. I'll give you—"

"Ten free questions to ask you." I pause before adding, "About your past."

He smiles. "If I win, I want the same. Agreed?"

"Sure," I nod reluctantly. No way out of this now. I want to know about my brother. Don't know why my past would be interesting to him though. He probably thinks that I like him or something. Yuck! That's creepy!

"Name?" He pulls Eddie over. "Eddie you're my witness. Right?"

Eddie nods.

I say the name of the only female in charge that I know. "Captain Via."

Oliver slams his fists into the desk. "How do you do that?"

Guess I was right. I win.

We only have one more night before we dock at the designated rendezvous point. It might be my last chance to collect my win. I hunt Oliver down to ask him the questions. We find a quiet place on the deck. The air is cold. Winter is coming and we cautiously travel more north in order to avoid the path of the "Queen Nalani" ship. I am bundled up in a blanket, seated on a chair on the deck. "Did you pick here because you think I'll freeze and give up before I get through all of the questions?"

"No." Oliver buttons up his jacket. "But *will* you?"

I shake my head. "First question. What do you remember about your life before the virus?"

"Not much. I remember that we were all hiding in a small house for a long time."

"Who?" I ask. "Who was hiding?"

"Second question is who was hiding? Well there was my father and me. A woman was with us for a short while. I assume she was my nanny. I don't remember much about her."

"I thought that was a part of the first question, but that's okay. What do you remember about the nanny?" My father never mentioned a nanny, but he did say my mother was with them before I disappeared. I have to believe that there was no nanny, only my mother. That has to be our mother he remembers. I want to know as much as I can about her.

"Why in the world would you want to know about my nanny? That makes no sense whatsoever." He clutches his jacket. He is not invincible. He's cold too.

"My questions and that is number three." I wrap the blanket tighter. "Tell me about the nanny."

"Okay, I'll play along." He shakes his head and sighs. "I haven't thought of her in a long time. She had hair the color of yours. She had a sweet smell."

I prod. "Anything else?"

He retorts. "Is that question four?"

"Yes." I reply.

He sits for a moment as if he is trying hard to remember her. "You know I do remember one thing. She had a heart."

"A heart, everyone has a heart."

"No she actually had a heart." He points to his neck. "She had a heart right here on her neck."

My stomach flutters and I gasp. "What kind of heart? A tattoo?"

"No, I'm not sure what it was, but I don't think it was a tattoo. It was red like a rash."

I hold my breath before letting it out slowly. "Could it have been a birthmark?"

He nods. "Yes, it could have been that. Strange that I

remembered that about her."

I can't talk. Could it be? But how could my mother still be alive? It can't be. I need to ask the last six questions carefully. I open my mouth to ask my next question, but I stop. I hear something in the distance. It's faint. "Do you hear that?"

Oliver slaps his leg. "What? The sound of you running out of questions?"

I throw off my blanket and slam my hand over his mouth. "No, listen."

We are silent for a few minutes. The sounds of the waves hitting into the side of the ship come at expected intervals. Oliver becomes as quiet as I am as we stand at the rail leaning over to trying to perk our ears to hear the voice. I don't want to have imagined it.

It's words, someone talking. A distinct voice. I cannot make out what it is saying, but it's definitely a person. "Don't you hear that?"

Oliver leans over the rail as far as he can. "I do." A few seconds later, he runs towards the ship's cabin. I throw off my blanket and dart after him.

Oliver reaches the cabin and slides open the door. "Captain. We heard someone out in the sea."

The captain shakes his head. "Probably Undesirables or Uncounteds thrown overboard." He walks out of the cabin and peers over the side. "I hope we can find them. It's so dark."

I ask, "What about shining a light out there?"

The captain shakes his head. "Not this close to shore."

I look around. "I'll take one of the life boats and go toward the sound."

Oliver frowns at me. "Are you crazy? It's too dangerous. You'll be killed!"

"What kind of people would we be, if we don't at least try?" I take off for the lifeboats before the captain or Oliver can stop me. I noticed the boats when I boarded the ship. I knew right where they were. All I had to do was to unhook the rope. Once that was done, the boat would automatically drop into the ocean. I dodge a couple of mates on the way and when I locate the lifeboat, I jump in and release the lever. The boat slides so quickly down that I fall into the end of the boat. I hear a thud about half way down and the boat rocks. Another person sits on the other side of the lifeboat. It's Oliver.

"You almost made the boat flip!" I yell at him.

He crouches as we splash into the water below. "I can't let you die." The boat heaves a few times before it steadies in the water.

I shake my head. "What about you?"

He grabs an oar and hands me another one. "They have to come after me. Remember I'm the ambassador's son and also I am the only one who can operate the communications."

I start pushing the oar back and forth. "You're risking your life to save me. Am I that good of an assistant?"

"Not at all." He laughs for a minute then stops. "For some reason I think you are worth saving."

"Why?" I ask.

"Because you're willing to jump in this dark water and risk death for people you've never met. I've never had a chance to be heroic. I want to try it, for once. Besides, it's the only way I could think of to make sure you survive."

I pull the oar through the water again. "What do you mean?"

He smirks, "They'll come after me, if I don't return. I'm kind of important."

I smile. "It may be the last thing you do."

"Hope not."

We feverishly push the oars through the open sea and the voices get louder.

"Look!" He shouts, "You were right."

In the distance, I spot a piece of wood with three people holding onto it. One of them, a male, yells. "Help!" It's faint, labored cry for help so we quickly steer our lifeboat toward them. We have to be in time to save them, we just have to be.

It's only a couple of moments before our lifeboat is perpendicular to the floating wood. The waves chop into the side of our boat causing it to almost capsize. We struggle to pull in the survivors into our boat. After losing the survivors back into the water a few times, Oliver and I finally manage to drag all three of them into the boat. I take off my jacket and Oliver does too. We try to cover them as much as we can. They are so quiet that I fear we might have been too late.

It takes a few minutes to row back to the ship. We are all lugged back on our pirate ship by our ship's mates and wrapped in blankets. The five of us are carried into the kitchen area. I throw off my blanket as the three survivors from the sea are stretched out on the long tables.

"Are they going to be okay?" I ask.

"Paisley?" The voice saying my name is one I recognize.

Chapter 23

There stretched out on the makeshift medical table in the kitchen is Riley. I can't contain myself. "Riley!" I throw my arms around him.

He groans. "Paisley!"

A woman yanks me off him. "Honey, you need to back off and let this boy breathe." She wipes his face and offers him water. He doesn't move. He stares at me. She hands me the water. "Do you want to see if you can get him to drink?'

I nod, draw him up, and lift the water to his mouth. He drinks a little at first, and then starts to gulp. "Not that fast. There's plenty. You're safe now, Riley."

I pull the necklace over my head and put it around his neck. "I think you need this more than me. You need its luck to make you better."

The woman rubs his hair and feels his forehead. "He needs to sleep. That'll make him better. Tomorrow we will get some food in him as soon as he wakes up. We should be in Bavaria."

I tear up. "Bavaria is our home."

She smiles. "Home always makes everything better."

I nod. Riley settles down holding tightly to my hand. As he drifts off, his grip loosens. I haven't thought to look at the other two people we dragged in. Maybe I know them. I walk slowly over to study their faces. I'm shocked when I realize that I do know one of them.

"Baako." I mutter.

Since Baako is here, does that mean that they caught him? Did he tell them about Colt? Where is Colt? I can't ask either Baako or Riley right now and the older woman is burned too badly to ask. What if Colt, Gretel, or my mother were thrown overboard also, but didn't survive?

At first, I fight sleep. I stare at them both waiting impatiently for either Riley or Baako to wake up and tell me what happened.

After a few hours, I lose the battle and fall asleep. I wake in the morning when I feel a hand brush through my hair. It's Riley. He's awake. He asks, "Have you been here all night?"

"Where is Gretel? What about Mom and Colt?" I rub the sleep out of my eyes. "Where are they?"

"They're all safe." He sits up taller. I let out a relieved sigh and hand him a cup of water.

"Not so fast," I chastise, when he gulps it once again. "You need to remember to take it in slow. I'll get you some food in a minute. Do you know what happened?"

He puts the cup down and looks around. "Did Baako make it?"

I nod and point over to the other table. "He's over there. What about the woman? Who is she?"

"Did she make it?" He shifts around.

"Yes," I answer. "They're taking care of her. Said she should be fine in a few days. Who is she?"

"Her name is Tury. She just ended up with us. I'm glad she made it." He dangles his legs over the side of the table. "When you left, I hid for days. Baako kept coming around looking for me. I finally found Colt and told him that you had run off after the princess recognized you. They looked for me until word came about the ambassador's death."

"What happened when they heard?"

"The queen and the princess went crazy. Colt had to

stay with them all the time. He has kind of taken over as a surrogate father to the princess."

I smile. That is so Colt. "Mom and Gretel?"

"He's been looking in on them from time to time. Gretel took the ambassador's death hard. The queen asked Gretel to stay with them since she was so close with the ambassador."

I frown. "So do they not realize that King Ahomana had the ambassador killed?"

"What are you talking about?" He shakes his head. "I don't think the king knew anything about it. From the talk around the ship, the king just wanted the ambassador jailed not killed. Someone else put the kill order on the ambassador. The king is behaving like he's been betrayed. He is *too* distraught that his daughter is so upset. I don't think there is any way he would have done something this diabolical and permanent to hurt his daughter. He loves her. He seems confused and paranoid. He's not doing well at all. He is allowing others to control. He hasn't even recognized Colt. Colt has an inside seat with the royals and he told me that they're all in shock."

I pull myself up and sit with him on the table. "If the king didn't have him killed then who did?"

Riley shakes his head. "I have an idea. It's a scary thought. I think there is a new heinous force to be reckoned with. An American Merc is now running the show. He knows the king is not thinking straight and has swooped in. That's why the queen is so protective of the princess now. **This Merc is trying to convince the queen that she needs him to protect them.** I heard a rumor that he is trying to marry her while she is in this weakened state. He's pushing hard to make it happen before the baby is born. He's power hungry. He wants to be a royal."

"Is she falling for that?" I scrunch my face up. "That's downright creepy."

He nods. "I'm afraid that she is. The queen wants someone to make sure that her family is safe. I'm worried." He lets out a deep sigh. "The only thing that Gretel and Colt can do is to watch out for the princess. They're doing a good job of that. I guess as soon as the new baby is born they'll take over watching that baby too."

I sigh. "What about Mom?"

He says, "Still in the kitchen. No change."

"What happened?" I look around. "Why did you three get thrown overboard?"

"You don't understand." He shakes his head. "We didn't get *thrown* overboard. We jumped."

I hit the floor and swing around facing him head on. "Why on earth would you jump off the ship?"

Baako lifts up and weakly says, "He did it for me."

"I don't understand." I turn back to Riley.

Riley nods. "He's right. I was hiding with this other woman, Tury. She's an Undesirable and would have been killed. She's been with me for a while now. Baako was bringing us food when a Merc caught him. The Merc was going to turn us all in. Baako would have been executed for treason."

I nod. "So you jumped."

Baako smiles. "We did get the wood we floated on before we jumped over. It was a door that they were replacing."

"I'm glad you made it." I put one arm around Riley's shoulder. "That was a dangerous thing to do. What's Colt going to think?"

Riley drops his head. "He's going to think we are *dead* when he can't find us."

I pull his chin up with my other hand and then hug him close. "Thankfully, you're not dead. Tomorrow we will be in Bavaria. Then we can join up with our army and defeat these Mercs once and for all."

"It'll take an army." Riley squeezes me back. "By the way, what kind of ship is this?"

"A pirate ship."

"Only you would find a pirate ship." He chuckles, pulls the necklace from around his neck, and hands it back to me. "This four-leaf clover is for you. You keep it for luck."

"I do love this necklace." I twirl the necklace in my hand for a second before I pull it back over my head. "It brought you luck. You're going to be okay."

"It'll be a long time before we are all okay, but at least I'm back with you. I was worried sick." He jumps off the table and stutters his stance for a moment before he steadies himself. "Right now, I'll take some food and maybe clean clothes."

I smile. "Right this way." I turn back to Baako. "Baako, you coming?"

Baako slides off the table. He stands over Tury and rubs her brow for a moment. "I'll stay with Tury to make sure she is okay."

"We'll bring food when we come back." I look at the woman taking care of them. "Make sure they're okay." The woman looks over at her patients. "She is sleeping now. He'll be fine. No hurry, take your time. I'll watch over them."

Riley and I walk out the door.

At the kitchen, we run into Oliver. "So you're the reason that Paisley jumped in the water."

Riley looks at me. "You jumped in the water?"

Oliver knocks his shoulder into mine. "She almost killed herself trying to save you."

I stammer, "I didn't know it was you. I just knew that someone was out in the water yelling."

Riley's face drops. "Oh."

I start again. "I didn't mean it like that..." I mumble. "...if I had known it was you...I would have..."

Riley cocks his head.

"I got nothing." I shake my head. "Sorry, but I would have jumped in the water to save whoever was in there. But I *am* glad it was you."

Riley chuckles. "So you're glad that I almost drowned."

I stare at him stone-faced. "I didn't mean that and you know it."

He smiles at me and then turns back to Oliver. "And you are?"

Oliver answers, "Oliver, Paisley has been working with me. We have been trying to reestablish communications with the resistance."

Riley stiffens and curtly asks, "Is that *all* you were working on?"

Oliver nonchalantly nods, oblivious to the tone of the question.

I think Riley is jealous. I like that. Unfortunately, I can't tell him that he has no reason to be jealous since Oliver is my brother because Oliver doesn't know that he is my brother. What a mess!

During dinner, Oliver tells Riley all about the communication system. He explains how we are connecting with all of the resistance factions from all over the world. He shares the plan to get the nations to vote for a democracy and end human trafficking.

Riley eats throughout Oliver's explanation and says, "Well now I know why Paisley is hanging out with you. She does love to get in the middle of the resistance and put herself in danger. She actually tried to take the place of everybody sentenced to die by execution by telling the king to only execute her. I know first-hand what Paisley is capable of."

Oliver leans back in his chair. "So where do you stand on all of this, Riley?"

Riley laughs and pats me on the back. "Right by Paisley. She has not steered me wrong yet. We are in this together." He cocks his head and stares at Oliver. "What's the plan?"

Oliver smiles. "Glad to hear that. I do have an idea and I'm going to need your help. We are going to the maze to recruit people willing to deliver portable communicators to every faction of the rebellion in all of Europe. We need to be able to talk to one another if we are going to organize a coup. I need you and Paisley to help me get in the maze."

Riley nods and I say, "We'll do it. That sounds great."

We spend the last day onboard working on the patches and make enough of them as a guide for others. The plan is to get close enough to the maze for Aunt Sandra's boys to find us. We'll share our ideas and give them the patches and communicators to pass out. Then we will be in touch with everyone so we will be able to coordinate a strike and wipe out the Mercs. It's a good strategy. I hope it works.

Eddie helps us pack up the portable communicators. Fortunately, they are so small we can take many in our backpacks along with the patches. The plan is to wait until nighttime to make our move so we'll be cloaked in darkness. When it's time Oliver, Riley, and I disembark on a lifeboat to shore. We journey through the woods to the designated rendezvous point. Being back on the European continent has its merits. The sights, sounds, tastes, and smells of home fill my soul and calm me.

We sit in the bushes for a couple of hours waiting for contact. I ask, "Oliver, why is it taking so long? Do you think something happened?"

He says, "No. They're being careful. These are the coordinates. Be patient."

Patience is not one of my virtues. I almost fall asleep when I hear rustling in the bushes. It's our contact. A young boy creeps up and says, "Roses are red and violets are blue."

Oliver smiles and says, "If you say this line, then I'll know it is you."

The boy motions to a trail. "I have horses waiting for us. They are only a couple of kilometers."

We all begin our trek down the path.

I catch up with the boy. "What's your name?"

"Josef." The boy slows his pace to match mine.

I ask, "What does PACO stand for?"

He takes in a deep breath. "I love telling this. There was a story about two brave young people who chose to give their lives to save others. Their names started with a pa and a co. Their names are Paisley and Colt."

I gasp.

Chapter 24

Josef turns to face me. "We came for you. We know you are one of the brave ones, Paisley. We know all about you. You are a legend. Everyone talks about you and Colt. We know that you are special."

Oliver leans over to Riley and I hear him whisper, "Is there anything that she is not involved in?"

Riley shakes his head and chuckles under his breath.

PACO, who knew?

Josef leads us down the trail to awaiting horses. I'm thrilled that one of the horses is my old friend, Hershey. I hug her, satisfying a piece of my heart. I am happy to have a few minutes to digest that they used our names for the resistance. We mount the horses, slip our feet into the stirrups, and set off.

It's strange to think of yourself as part of a legend. As we travel through the German terrain, Josef regales us with stories of my and Colt's adventures or misadventures. And as is always the custom, the stories are exaggerated the more they are told. I know some of these are the stories that Colt and I told the other SCs and Aunt Sandra's comrades. They are so altered now, they don't even sound like the same stories.

The story about the train ride has been embellished to include a run across the tracks with us beating up a conductor and saving all of the people on the train. The rescue of the Bavarian farm people at the train station has been inflated to include an all out gun battle with an army of guards and the fib that got us on the ship has been amplified to the point that we invented the Sponsored Companions program to make our way onto the ship.

As Josef is telling us these stories, I try to explain the truth, but he doesn't listen.

Oliver leans over after Josef refuses to listen once again. "People like to have heroes. What's the harm in the stories being more exaggerated than they actually were? You are giving hope to a large contingent of children who are fighting and possibly dying for this cause. Nothing is more inspiring than someone who actually was courageous. You were brave in all of these instances, right?"

I nod. I guess he has a point. How can we convince anyone to take up arms and battle through this fight if they don't believe it can be won? What better way than to have a story about someone or in this case two someones who actually did just that. I guess a little embellishment won't hurt.

"Look!" Josef points out a tree with the letters PACO carved into it. "See I told you, you're famous!"

Riley chuckles, as I turn red. Nothing like a little embarrassment to make the time go faster.

"Where are we going?" I ask as we round a trail high in the hills. We travel most of the day and I still have no idea where we are heading.

Mike rides up. "Always so impatient."

I'm startled for a moment; I haven't seen Mike since we were at the Ferris wheel farm. But the sight of one of our farm children makes my heart sing. I can't help but smile. No bandages or slings this time. I ask, "Your leg is all healed? I guess falling off that Ferris wheel wasn't as bad as we first thought."

He nods as Thomas rides up behind him and dismounts.

I jump off Hershey. "Thomas, it's great to see you. It seems like being put in charge has agreed with you and Mike." I reach up my hand and touch the top of his head. "You've grown a half a meter."

Thomas stands as tall as he can. I am bursting with pride. I take comfort that we left our children of the farm in good hands.

Hershey nuzzles me. "Hershey, wish I had an apple to give you."

Thomas pulls an apple out of his pack and tosses it to me. "Here, but hurry. The Mercs still patrol here and we have about another hour before we are completely safe."

I feed Hershey quickly and mount again. The hour on the trail is spent filling Thomas and Mike in about how Colt and my family are still on the ship set to dock in a couple of days and how Colt is looking out after the princess and the queen since the ambassador's death. Thomas asks how Colt managed to impersonate a Merc. Riley explains it with the story about the switch and the storeowner.

"There are a lot of people like that storeowner on our side." Mike pats his horse and points to a turn on the trail. "We'll be safe from here. This part of the trail is not marked and is guarded by us all of the time."

"How do you know if people are on your side?" Oliver asks.

"It's guesswork now." Mike sighs.

Oliver lights up. "That's where we can help." He pulls out a patch. "We've made these patches so we can easily identify the resistance and those on our side. We've also developed a portable communicator. We plan to get information to every underground station that we know of. We'll give each of these groups extra communicators and patches so they can pass them out. We want this rebellion to succeed with as little bloodshed as possible."

Mike nods. "I agree there's been enough death." He sighs. "There's something you don't know, Paisley."

Riley crouches on his horse to avoid a tree branch. "Nothing bad, I hope."

"No." Thomas grasps the reins of Hershey, my horse. "Whoa! We're almost there. Maybe Aunt Sandra should tell her." He looks over at Mike.

Mike nods. "Maybe."

I ask, "Tell me what?"

Mike turns and faces me. "They want you to be the new face of the Consortium of the World since the ambassador is dead. We need someone to represent hope."

"Me?" I feel the blood seeping out of my face slithering down to my toes. I'm not a leader. I'm just a farm girl from Bavaria. What would I know about inspiring a movement? I haven't even turned sixteen yet. That doesn't make sense. How would I represent hope?

Mike dismounts. "We're here. We'll talk about it later."

The rest of us dismount and leave the horses in a guard's care. I recognize the beginning of the maze into Aunt Sandra's realm. It takes about half an hour to make our way through the cave, then through the maze before we reach the inner sanctum. I am relieved when I glimpse the top of the castle. Just the sight of the castle gives me a warm feeling all over.

Aunt Sandra, Kelley, and Amanda are there to greet us. We are led to a long table full of food.

"Don't have to ask me to eat. I'm starving." I grab a piece of bread and bite off a corner. "What's this about me being a face for democracy?" I direct my question to Aunt Sandra. "What about you? Why can't you be the face?"

"My place is here." Aunt Sandra picks up a tomato, cuts it in two with a knife, and puts it on a serving plate. "You and Colt are the catalysts that started this whole movement. You need to be the face of freedom."

Oliver picks up the half of tomato and tosses it in his mouth. "I have to agree. Studying history teaches us that we need to have some ideal or someone to follow. The Americans have the ambassador and since everyone thought you were dead, you became the martyr for this side of the world. Everyone over here followed your ideals. We all have to have heroes."

Aunt Sandra pats Oliver's hand. "I was sorry to hear about your father."

Oliver nods for a moment. "Thanks." It's strange how I

seem to be more upset about our father's death than he is. I shouldn't judge though, I don't know what he's been through.

After dinner, Oliver shares the portable communicators explaining how they work to Aunt Sandra and to a few of her top allies. He also shows her the broken egg patch. I explain to her how to make it so it can be destroyed in a matter of seconds if the wearer is caught.

"Ingenious." Aunt Sandra announces, "Tomorrow morning, we will begin disseminating the portable communicators and instructions on how to make the patches to the rest of our resistance cells. You should make contact with your shop owner. I'm sure she will know of others."

I light up. "Do you think the "Queen Nalani" ship will be there by then?"

Aunt Sandra nods. "It probably will. But Colt and your family are safe for now. You need to stay on plan and not deviate. Do you understand?"

Riley stands up. "She doesn't understand how to follow the rules, but I do. I'll make sure the plan is carried out."

Riley is always looking out for me whether I want him to or not.

That night, I toss and turn. I'm so restless it's almost impossible to fall asleep. My mind is racing with thoughts about all of the things that can go wrong with our plan. All of the people that can be hurt or killed. I can't stop my mind from running one disastrous scenario after another.

I'm worried about my family. **What will become of them? They don't even know I survived. They must still think I am back in America.** What if they try to go back and find me? I can't possibly know the answer to any of this so I work myself up into a dither, but the good thing about dithers is that you eventually fall asleep.

The next morning we set out to put our plan in action.

The trail is long and arduous, but we finally make it to Hamburg. There sits the "Queen Nalani" ship. It takes everything I have not to run down the street and get on board, screaming at the top of my lungs, "Gretel, Colt and Mom, I'm alive! I'm here!"

Instead, we enter the Sponsored Companions doll shop. The only change in the shop is the addition of a few more posters of new Sponsored Companions. Seeing no living beings in the store to be sold, I can only guess that the living dolls are bought as soon as they arrive. Behind the desk sits a familiar face. Her features are not as chiseled as they were before, her lips are pursed, gray streaks throughout her hair, lines crevasse her face making her look more worn than the last time we saw her.

"Hello, Ms. DeVane," Riley blurts out as we walk in.

Taken by surprise, she gasps and stands. It takes her a moment to gain her composure. Her eyes dart surveying the room. "Follow me."

She leads us to the back where we catch up on what has been going on. She asks about her son and we tell her that we haven't found any information about him yet, but we're still looking.

Oliver props his elbows on the table. "I can find out about your child. Give me his full name and month and day of birth."

Ms. DeVane trembles. "William DeVane. October 26."

Oliver takes out a device. It's not like the communicator; it's smaller with a key pad.

"What's that?" I ask.

"It's a portable computer. I have it hooked up to the mainframe back in America. I'm connected to satellites that have been orbiting our planet since before the virus. As we travelled across the ocean, I re-connected this continent with America." The computer beeps. "Here it is."

Ms. DeVane gasps. "You found him? How?"

Oliver holds up the computer. "I've been collecting information for months. I began this database while I was working on the computer project. I've been inputting the information so we can find our loved ones. I realized early on that most people just want to know where their families are. Once reunited, we can find safe places for them. Many people work with me to help find others and free them."

Ms. DeVane's voice cracks and tears run down her face. "Where's my boy?"

Oliver turns the computer's screen to face Ms. DeVane so she can read it. "He is in a camp in Frankfurt, Germany. He is assigned as a horse trainer." A grin encompasses Oliver's face. "This is the best part of my job. We'll be going through there. We'll find him and see what we can do then." He writes down the information he shared on a piece of paper and hands it to Ms. DeVane.

Ms. DeVane holds the note like a fragile egg. "Thank you. Thank you so much." She throws her arms around Oliver's shoulders.

"This is how we will defeat our enemies by bringing families back together. We'll become strong and democracy will follow." Oliver places his computer back in his bag.

"I had no idea you had something like that." I shake my head at Oliver. "That's amazing."

"Me neither." Riley says. "That device would be very dangerous in the wrong hands. It must be protected."

A voice from the front of the store announces, "That's why we're here."

Chapter 25

It's Lieutenant Drake. He saved Colt and me when we first came to Hamburg. I'm glad to see that he survived and even though he looks like a man not used to physical contact, I hug him. "I was wondering if we would ever see you again."

He hesitates for a moment, but squeezes me back picking me up a little off the floor. "You are quite different now. Back when I first we met you, you had an awful stench about you."

I giggle. "You're being nice, we smelled awful. I never got a chance to thank you."

"Save your thanks," He places me back on the floor and points to the back door. "Because I am going to get you out of a tight spot again."

"What are you talking about?" I regain my footing.

"We were told you were coming here. We came to take you to a safe place. Follow me." He walks toward the back door.

Ms. DeVane clasps my hand. "Take some of the new outfits and put them in your backpacks you might need them later. You know how to pass as a Sponsored Companion."

"Thanks." I embrace her and grab a handful of the new Sponsored Companion outfits as we leave. Fortunately, the hat and clothes are packaged together. I quickly shuffle through the shoeboxes to find our right sizes. I find a copy of the tattoo we need and throw it in the bag too. Could come in handy later.

Riley holds the back door open as we three, along with Lieutenant Drake, exit. Riley asks, "Why the rush? Has something happened?"

"Yes." Lieutenant Drake holds up a newspaper. "The Consortium of the World negotiations have been put on hold and King Ahomana has been put in charge."

I grab the paper and there he is, King Ahomana sitting on the throne in all his glory. "They voted? I didn't hear about a vote."

"No vote, but that doesn't matter now." Lieutenant Drake points to the man beside the king in the picture. "This man is our real problem. The king's second in command is Emperor Richard the Great. He doesn't follow any rules."

Riley asks, "What does this mean?"

"I've heard from a variety of reliable sources that this emperor has his sights set on ruling the world. He doesn't want a vote. He just wants to take over." The lieutenant sighs. "My guess is that the king will be assassinated in the next few weeks and that the emperor will be in charge. Unfortunately if that happens, all this talk about negotiating democracy and the Consortium of the World will be just that—talk."

I question fervently, "What about the queen and the princess? What will happen to them?"

The lieutenant shakes his head. "No idea, but we need to get you to a safe place *immediately*."

We follow the lieutenant through the winding back alleys and streets until we come to a dilapidated clock store. We remove a couple of boards out of the way to enter. Inside the shop, we uncover a hidden door to stairs that lead underground. Once there, lanterns light the way. The corridor of the cavern is about half a kilometer long. At the mouth of the cave is another entrance into another store. We enter it and hide its existence by positioning a crate over it.

Lieutenant Drake opens the inner door. "Stay here for now so we can coordinate our plan."

"We already have a plan. We have orders of what to do." I protest. "We're supposed to go around and pass out these communicators and patches to our allies."

"My men and I will do that. You are much too valuable to be out in the open."

I stand with my hands on my hips. "If I'm that valuable, then what about Colt?"

"I knew you would say that!" Drake smiles. "We are executing a plan right now to free him from the ship."

"No, you can't! He's protecting my mom and Gretel and the princess!" I shriek.

"Quiet! Someone will hear you!" Drake covers my mouth with his hand. "I'm sorry, but Colt's safety takes precedence over your family."

I struggle to free Drake's grip. I mumble through his hand, but my muffled sounds don't make any sense. My eyes search out Riley. I know he reads my desperation. Riley lunges at Drake, but is quickly subdued by others in the store that we now inhabit.

I jerk my head free and furiously spout at Drake. "Are we *your* prisoners now?"

"Sorry. You have to stay put." Drake shakes his head. "There is no other way."

I rock back and forth with my head in my hands. Colt won't go without a fight. He will make them save Gretel. He won't leave her, I just know it.

The night is long. We aren't allowed to move or talk or do anything. Finally, the door opens and there stands Gretel.

"Gretel!" I squeal and run to her.

She yells, "Paisley, you made it! You're alive!"

I hug her tightly. "Where's Mom and Colt?"

She pulls from my grip and motions toward the door. A man carrying Colt walks in the door and says, "He wouldn't leave without her. We had to bring them both."

Drake slams his fist on the table. "Did we lose any?"

The man shakes his head. "No, Colt fought them off. He took a couple of bullets."

Gretel orders them: "Find a flat place, table, floor, anything. I need to get the bullets out now and sew him up before he loses anymore blood."

Drake brushes plates and cups off the table and asks, "Are you a doctor?"

Two of the men hoist Colt onto the table.

"Close as you're going to get. Find alcohol, sewing needle, and knife. If you have it, bring something to dull his pain." She rips Colt's shirt off. "A very sharp razor would be a big help."

Gretel barks more orders. "Bandages or something to use as bandages. Boil some water, a bowl of clean water, and rags. I'm going to need thread and a pair of scissors."

People scurry about finding the items or locating suitable replacements.

Gretel works quickly. "I have to get the bullets out and sanitize the area so it doesn't get infected." She cuts into Colt's midsection. "Looks like the bullets lodged into your muscle. It'll be painful, but you should survive." She digs for the two bullets with the knife. "Sorry Colt, this isn't too pretty and it's going to hurt." She sighs loudly. "A lot."

Colt groans. "Do what you have to. I trust you."

I stand silently, attempting to guess what she will need. I hand her a knife, rags, and water. I try to sop up the blood as the gash widens. As soon as one rag is red with blood, I get another.

Colt moans and grits his teeth the whole time she is prodding. Blood gushes out the deeper she goes. The rags are soaked with his blood by the time she retrieves the bullets. As Gretel jabs, she stops for a moment. "I'm sorry." Tears run down her face and I wipe her cheeks as fast as I can.

Colt manages a meek, "I'm okay."

"Scissors?" Gretel asks me.

I search around and shake my head.

"No scissors, huh?" Gretel looks around the table and picks up the alcohol. "This is going to hurt, but I have to sanitize the wound."

She pours alcohol onto his gash and he yelps in pain.

Gretel swallows a sob, sets the alcohol down, and holds out her hand. "Needle and thread."

I locate the items. She threads the needle and douses the needle and thread with alcohol before starting her work. Colt clenches his fists, groaning the whole time as she sews him up.

When she finishes, Gretel bites the thread with her teeth. "With no scissors, it's the best I could do." She dabs his wound with a clean rag, sopping up the blood.

Colt grabs her hand and whispers, "Thanks. I love you."

She wraps his torso with a bandage and then kisses his forehead. "I couldn't live without you, remember that."

Blood drains from Colt's face and he passes out. Gretel's face is filled with fear until she takes his pulse and breathes a sigh of relief. "Let him rest, he'll be better in the morning." She walks over to the faucet and runs water over her hands, rinsing off blood. She spends a lot of time scrubbing her hands. The blood is gone, but she keeps cleaning them. She's in shock. I know she is used to seeing blood, but this is Colt's. It's different.

I hug her again. "What about Mom?"

Gretel shakes her head. "She was in the kitchen. We couldn't get to her. I am sure they don't know who she is. She should be fine, but we do need to get her off that ship."

I nod. "We'll worry about that later. At least your both alive and here out of harm's way."

She glances towards the table holding Colt. "It's his birthday today. He's eighteen. Happy birthday to him. What away to spend it."

Eighteen. He's a man now. He proved it. The first thing he did as a man was to refuse to leave his love behind even if it meant his own death. I will always love him for that.

Drake looks over Colt and then slides a chair over for Gretel to sit on. "You did a good job on him." He flips a chair around and sits in it backwards. "What's going on with the royals?"

Gretel fills us in. "The new second in command, Emperor Richard, is manipulating the queen. The queen is weak because of the pregnancy. The emperor has been pushing the queen to marry him. He tells her it's because he wants her and her children to be safe, but he wants to make himself a royal by marriage. We can't let that happen."

I agree with Gretel.

It feels good to have Gretel, Colt, and Riley all in one place. Now if we can only get my mom to safety. Not to mention my birth family. Fortunately, my brother Oliver is with me, but the princess and her unborn sibling are on that ship and in the enemy's hands.

It seems so hopeless.

Colt sleeps with Gretel's head resting on his hand. I sit on a chair beside Gretel touching her arm with my finger.

It takes hours for everyone to regain their composure. No one is allowed to leave. I want to go to my mom, but Drake refuses to let me. I am imprisoned for days in the makeshift center of command in Hamburg while Oliver and Drake organize supporters to deliver the communicators and the patch with the guide on how to make it.

Oliver runs diagnostics daily on the communicators. It is through these sessions that we find out our grassroots efforts are making an impact. It only takes a couple of days before we begin to receive messages from cells of resistance all over the globe. I'm angry that I'm not allowed to try to free my mom, but I do see progress every day.

Riley draws a large map of the world and hangs it on the wall. Every time we make contact with a cell, Riley notes it on the map with a colored stickpin. In two weeks, we have most of the map covered. In addition, I have been inventorying the amount of supporters located in each faction. Our numbers grow daily.

With this new information, I am optimistic.

Hope is spreading. The mood is more positive. We gather daily to read the propaganda being disseminated by those who want to remain in control.

The more followers the resistance gains, the more heinous the actions of the Mercs become. Mercs have ruled using fear for so long that they think they can continue to scare everyone into submission. Every day someone is executed for treason. If caught, we will be executed too. Riots break out in the streets. Riley and Oliver try to calm the factions using the communicators. The resistance is told of how many supporters there are and asked to be patient. Our time will come. But it is hard for me to be patient so I know it must be impossible for them. Especially those in the outlying areas. How can they possibly see what we see? All they know is that their food supply is dwindling and there doesn't seem to be anyone to save them from their only two options, a life as a servant or certain death.

Nightly, Colt and I transmit a program called, "Speak to the Troops." It's aimed at keeping morale high. We tell our stories with embellishments that make them so much more interesting. Riley shares his Merc status in an attempt to garner support from disgruntled Mercs. Oliver speaks as the voice of the fallen ambassador. He doesn't identify himself, but only says he served with the ambassador. He fears that if he reveals his true identity, the princess and queen might be in danger. No one wants a little girl or a pregnant mother to die, not even the troops. Drake says scouts report Mercs are scouring the countryside looking for the source of the transmissions.

The goriest is the list of those executed. We received word that there is to be a televised execution, the first ever. Emperor Richard plans to use this spectacle to launch his rhetoric and spread his lies. Our group attempts to shut down the broadcast, but are unsuccessful.

Oliver rigs up a makeshift television so we can capture the signal and view the execution. No one wants to watch it, but we need to keep up to date with what is going on with the Mercs and the emperor.

Gretel and I choose not to observe such a heinous act until I hear Colt. "Don't let the two girls back in here."

It must be someone I know. I bolt through the door and Gretel follows.

On the screen, people are lined up with guns pointed at

them. Riley grabs me as I enter the room. "Go back. You don't want to see this."

I recognize almost all of their faces from the ship. They are the Undesirables and Uncounteds. What an atrocious act! I shake my head and bury it into his chest. He's right, I don't want to watch this.

I can hardly hear anything for my own sobbing. One shriek pierces the air loud and clear.

It's my sister. "Not Mom! No!"

Chapter 26

The shots ring out and the thumping sounds of crumpling humans permeate through the television. Gretel and I grab each other and clutch the sides of the small screen screaming together "No!" to no avail. Riley pulls me to him and grips me tightly. I see out of the corner of my eye that Colt has grabbed a sobbing Gretel. My legs give way and Riley holds me up with his arms. I black out for a second. It's too much pain to bear. I can't believe what I just witnessed. Our beautiful mother who never did anything to anyone has been shot for no apparent reason except for the fact that they could shoot her. Painful sensations surge throughout into my body. I force my eyes to watch the television.

My blood boils as I see the Emperor Richard laughing. He addresses the camera and menacingly warns, "This is what happens if you don't obey your king."

My stomach roils. Sickness. I need to vomit, but I control it. Thanks goodness the princess is not on the deck to witness all of this. Her sweet innocent nature could not take it. The king is not even on the deck. How could this be? Has the Emperor Richard taken over completely?

I protect my heart as best I can. My insides are mush. I

don't feel like I can go on. My mother is gone and there is nothing I can do to bring her back. I dig deep. I must overcome this. I'll save this horror for a later date. I must resist the temptation to let it seep into my consciousness. I can't let this define me, I have to let it make me stronger. It's what my mother would have wanted. If only—I stop myself. I could go forever with if onlys and none of those if onlys would bring my sweet mother back. The only thing I can do at this point is honor her memory by making sure these tyrants are out of power.

I'm tired of being told what to do. "Drake, it's time we did something about this!"

Drake trembles as a tear rolls down a deep wrinkle on his cheek. He wipes it off with the back of his hand. Visibly shaken by what he saw, he asks, "What do you suggest?"

I shut my eyes to conjure up a viable plan. The few moments of silence allows me to clear my head. I experience a pure moment of clarity, which launches a diabolical thought. I know what exactly what we need to do.

"Hit them where it hurts. We need to cause mayhem and destruction!" I slam my fist on the table.

Drake walks over to me. "I know that you want to kill every last one of them, but some of them can be saved. We can't go blood for blood—"

"You don't know me very well, Lieutenant Drake, but that's not what I have in mind."

He sits at the table. "Then tell me."

"We need to destroy them from within. Make sure they cannot regain power."

He scrunches his eyes. "You've got my attention. I'm listening."

I explain, "I systematically will outline a series of events that will cause their downfall. I'll share my plan to destroy the regime from within. First, you need to understand the idea." I ask, "What do they fear most?"

Somebody yells out, "Loss of power."

I point to the stick pinned map. "More than that, they fear death. What if we start by making them believe the virus has reappeared?"

"Won't work." Riley shakes his head. "They'll know it's not true."

Colt joins in. "We could communicate with the resistance and tell them to bury—"

"Bury anything." Riley turns and faces Colt. "It's the fear. That might work. It doesn't matter what they bury." Riley offers. "Dead horses, farm equipment, whatever. The fear of the outbreak is all we need. We need graves. They can be empty. It's the fear that will push them into hiding."

I add, "They will clump together to ride out the storm. Then we stop their supply runs. We steal what they have. Eventually they will have to come to us. Then, they will die."

"Are you planning on slaughtering them?" Gretel asks, "Aren't we as bad as the Mercs then?"

I let out a long breath. "We're not going to be killing people who don't deserve it."

Gretel swallows a sob, "No one deserves to die. It must be peaceful. When we have them cornered, they must be allowed to surrender. We have to try for a peaceful solution."

I shake my head. "No, we kill them!" I yell, "Kill them all!"

Gretel pulls my face toward her face and stares at me in the eyes. "I'm feeling what you're feeling. I lost what you lost. Remember, we want to change the world. We want to get the bad people out of power. We don't want to become the bad people." A tear rolls down her cheek. "What would Mom want us to do?"

I jerk away. I want them dead. I want them all dead. I want it more than anything. But my sister who has just witnessed our mother's execution doesn't feel the same way. I fight what I feel in every atom in my body, a murderous contempt flowing through my veins. My world moves in slow motion. I curse Gretel under my breath.

I heave with arduous breath. Finally, my harsh and laborious breathing begins to slow. Right this minute, I really want to be a killer, but I know I'm not. I want to hold onto this hate, but I know I can't. I curse Gretel once more before I force my soul to give in to her better judgment. She is always my moral compass.

I take in a last deep breath, calm myself, and embrace my sister. "I hate it. I hate the fact that you're right, Gretel. When that time comes we will allow them to surrender." She is right and I know it. Plus, I know my mother would not want me to turn into a cold-blooded killer. She would have never condoned senseless murder. I need to keep my mother in my mind, not for revenge's sake, but so I will remember the difference between what is right and what is wrong.

We put our plan in motion. We monitor the chatter for days. Rumors of mass graves and return of the virus spread through the regions much like the actual virus. Before long, there is a panic. The roads once peppered by patrolling Mercs are deserted. With the Mercs retreating, we are able to move our rescued people more easily. Our base of operations is the hub for all communications. As fears swell, hopes for a resistance win increases.

Newspapers try their best to squash the dire reports, but it is hard to stop a rumor's momentum once it is started. Paranoia grows. Gretel synthesizes a virus immunization using my blood just in case the Mercs decide to actually reintroduce the real virus. Wins for our side accumulate.

Through the communicators, Riley and Colt locate our original farm group. They are relieved to find out they survived. Riley travels to see them and reunites with his family. Colt is able to talk with his mom and dad through the communicators that Oliver has provided. The farm group has been in the Alps hiding in a series of caves. Fortunately, severe weather kept the Mercs away. The original group hasn't lost too many. The ones who did perish died of old age. The group even boasts three new births.

It is decided that Riley will return to Hamburg along with Colt's mother and father. The rest of the farm group will stay to lead the Alps region of Europe toward democracy. Riley is a renewed and energized person when he returns after seeing his family. If Riley and his family can pick up like the last twelve years never happened, then there is hope for all of the regions. Oliver was right, the key is to put people back with their loved ones. Riley didn't even need to stay with his family, he just needed to know they were alive and that they still loved him.

Hope is a virus that we want to spread.

Another person they add to their number is William, Ms. DeVane's son. Ms. DeVane closes her shop and is smuggled out of the Hamburg to join William's group as it travels to southern Bavaria near the Passau area. All indications are that the group is doing well.

Everything is going our way until one day we get the newspaper and read that the queen has married the **second in command Merc, Emperor Richard, in a secret ceremony.**

Lieutenant Drake shakes his head. "It's only a matter of time before Richard kills the king. We thought the king was bad. If the emperor is in charge, we will *all* be in trouble. Life as we know it will cease to exist."

Chapter 27

It takes a few days to let what happened sink in. Our plans to thwart the regime are still in play, but a maniacal emperor is leading the royals. The emperor has renamed himself King Emperor Richard the Great and has publically professed his undying love and support of the princess and queen. The people don't know any better and follow his lead without question.

News is released that the queen gives birth. She, her new baby, and the princess are kept on the ship "Queen Nalani" as a safety precaution.

No one knows if any of this is true. There are rumors she is dead because no one has seen her in such a long time. It is reported that the new baby is a boy named Ross in honor of the ambassador. That news makes me cringe. I hate the fact that the Mercs are using my family and the love everyone had for the ambassador to further their own agenda.

I find Oliver sitting at the computer one morning looking particularly forlorn. "What are you thinking about?"

He turns away from the monitor to face me. "I know my father is dead. I should hate the queen, but the princess and the new prince are my family. They are my half-brother and my half-sister."

I sit silently by him not knowing what to say. I understand more than he can know. Oliver is my full brother so I feel exactly the same way that he does. I fight the urge to tell him the truth. I tell myself that he has enough on his mind without worrying about a long lost sister that he doesn't remember.

I could turn his world upside down by revealing what I now suspect: our mother is Captain Via of the American resistance. How many people with my same color eyes, same hair color have a heart-shaped birthmark on their neck? Not many. In addition, I do remember her looking at the picture of Oliver and sighing. Plus, she was inconsolable when she found out the ambassador was dead.

My mother. No, she would be my birth mother. My real mother died at the hands of a monster. A monster I plan to stop. It's impossible to keep my mind on the plan when I think about that horrific fiend so I push all of those feelings deep into the crevasses of my thoughts. I will deal with those wounds later after the battle is over and our side is victorious.

It seems that some good is coming out of all this. Colt and Gretel have decided to get married. Colt, Gretel, Riley, and I plan to travel back to the Aunt Sandra's compound. There is a church on the grounds and Aunt Sandra will perform the ceremony. We have done as much as we can from the city of Hamburg. Oliver will have to finish here and then join us at Aunt Sandra's compound before the wedding.

The next few days we travel back through familiar territory. It's nice to get out from that cramped store and breathe the brisk air of Bavaria. Spring is here and the mountains are green, freshly nourished from the melting snow. It revives me.

I watch Gretel and Colt bask in the love they have for each other. It will be a joyous time and that is exactly what is needed around here.

Colt and Gretel make their announcement on our "Speak to the Troops" nightly program. The happy news revitalizes the resistance and they have been getting all kinds of wedding wishes sent to them via the underground.

The resistance has reached into all of the continents. With the virus scare, we have forced most of the Mercs into hiding.

It is only a matter of time before we defeat them; but for now, I have a wedding to attend.

The weather couldn't be lovelier. The children have decorated the castle with local canola flowers that bloom wild in Germany. Aunt Sandra fashioned a white dress befitting a princess for Gretel to wear.

The ceremony is beautiful. Candles light their way. Gretel's radiant beauty engulfs the room. Love encircles the service. Everyone is here. Riley and I stand up for the bride and groom. I'm dressed in a deep blue dress. Yellow canola flowers are strategically placed throughout my hair.

As I walk down the aisle, I see Riley at the end of the walkway. My brother, Oliver, is sitting in the front row. My heart is full.

I am happy. I follow Amanda and Kelley down the path, a makeshift straw bed with flowers on each side. Colt beams as his parents walk with him. What a wonderful thing for Gretel to be able to gain this entire family all at once. She and Colt deserve to be happy.

I know many of the leaders of the rebellion cells requested a chance to attend, but having us all in one place was too dangerous. Two of our farm's army children, Thomas and Mike, wanted to attend; but it was decided that it was more important for them to head back to the Ferris wheel farm to gather the few residents still in training there. Too bad, more couldn't have been here to watch this profession of love.

My sister glows as she promises to love Colt for the rest of her life. He promises the same back and I believe them. I know Colt has loved my sister since they were children. How many people have a love like that? Over the past year, they have each risked and saved the other's life more times than I can count.

Today in this beautiful place, the world and nature

smile upon them as if placing its blessing of their union. The sun shines brighter than it usually does and the sky glows the most beautiful color shining like the blue emerald of the oceans in the picturesque postcards that decorate the kiosks. The weather is cool and crisp without a hint of tension. A perfect day!

Love is truly in the air. The two of them plan to stay at the maze compound for their honeymoon. Colt's dad and mother will travel back to lead the southern German rebellion cell. The lull in Merc activity has allowed the cells to thrive.

The festivities that follow are a part of the biggest party I've ever seen. Dancing and laughter fill the air. The war raging outside these walls is not allowed in. The invited want change, demand fairness, and hope for the return of democratic rule. People dancing and singing at this party are the real heroes. Those who sacrifice everything for a better way of life. I stand proud to be counted among them. My pride bursts as I watch my sister and new brother melt into one another on the dance floor.

I'm celebrating too. In a short while, I will return to my Ferris wheel farm for a quick visit. I draw my intensity from the massive giant and the land it inhabits, my farm, my home. If I am to be the positive face of the resistance, I must collect all of the strength I can muster. Colt has his reason for fighting. He has Gretel. I search for my strength. Thomas and Mike left a day ago and I'll travel after the ceremony to join them. Thinking about touching the earth on my farm reenergizes me.

Here at the maze compound, Oliver has used his time wisely, setting up a central communication hub. Colt and I are still the face of the rebellion. We go on the waves nightly for "Speak with the Troops." Fighting is at an all time high, and I want to go home one last time before my job gets even busier. There is no way to know how long the battle will last. Going home was my one request. My request was granted since I have done everything that has been asked of me and have been a good soldier. I am ecstatic to be traveling back to the farm. I wish that Riley could come with me, but he has to stay on the maze compound to train the troops. Oliver is returning to

Hamburg.

I smile and pet Hershey. "We're going home, old friend." He tosses his mane. It makes me think he understands me. I squeeze his side, causing him to quicken his pace.

I'm ready to drink in my home.

I can't wait.

Chapter 28

Eddie and Baako accompany me back to the farm. I'm in a hurry. They attempt to trot a slow speed, but end up galloping in sporadic intervals to keep up. The two of them are assigned to take care of me. I roll the four-leaf clover in my hand. What a lucky charm it has turned out to be. On the ride to my farm, I find myself missing Riley. So strange, I've hardly been away from him for a couple of hours, but I miss him so much I ache.

We spend our day traveling through the farmland by horse. I savor every minute of the trip and look for those things I recognize. We even go by the ravine where the Mercs used to dispose of their kills. I place flowers and say a prayer. It's the least that I can do.

My heart skips a beat when we arrive at the outskirts of my farm's land. I don't see the Ferris wheel until we round the corner. There it is—the magnificent metal giant, my Ferris wheel.

A child, Parker, runs out to us as we trot onto my land. "You're back, Paisley!" He is one of the younger ones. He's filled out nicely. His face has a look beyond his years. So sad the children had to grow up so quickly. I dream of a future when children will have time to play and just be children.

Parker pets Hershey as I dismount. He says, "Thomas and Mike said you were coming." He sways back and forth. "I told them I didn't believe them."

"Where are Arlas and the others?" I ask.

"They didn't make it." Another child walks up behind Parker. It's Finn. I didn't recognize him. Finn says, "We buried them in the back. I'll take you."

I walk with Finn and Parker. It's so sad. Would they have survived if I'd stayed? I'll never know. I visit the graves of the Undesirables and the Uncounteds who died on this farm trying to save these children.

It seems weird to be able to travel through our lands unencumbered. The fear about the virus has indeed put the entire world back in quarantine. All except us, that is, since we know the truth.

We still have to overthrow the regime and save the princess and new baby prince from the bloodthirsty King Emperor Merc, Richard the Great. What a joke! He is not great at all. He is pure evil. My fear is that the emperor thinks he is invincible and will stop at nothing to gain complete and total power. It has been discussed that he will kill not only the king and queen, but also the princess and the new little prince.

None of us can let that happen. We must take back the world and make it a place where no one will live in fear. It's a grand goal, but one I plan on achieving. Not on my own, but with help. It's worth the sacrifice. I know it and everyone else on our side does too.

I pull at my four-leaf clover bulleted necklace. I am glad that Eddie and Baako are with me. Gretel and Colt would not have been much company. They went on their honeymoon right after the ceremony.

I wish they could have gotten off the compound, but Aunt Sandra found them a place in the far reaches of her land where they could have some alone time. They have been incommunicado ever since. If they are not careful, we'll be having a little prince or princess of our own. I smile as I think of a little baby running around the maze.

I walk with great anticipation to the Ferris wheel to take

my ride. I always wanted to cut my way out of this world. Is the world we've made now any better than the one we came from? Are we better off? We have to be.

It's scary to think about what the world will be like if we allow the Mercs or the emperor to take over. Right now, servants are uprising and leaving their owners. The rich are having a hard time fending for themselves. They don't know how to get their own food or take care of their own needs. They've always had someone doing that for them. It's a change for them and one they're not equipped to handle. It's funny how none of the riches in the world can buy good health. The wealthy are desperately trying to buy a guarantee that they will not contract the virus.

A big secret is that Gretel shared with us is that the ambassador developed the vaccine before his death and gave the formula to Gretel. We are fortunate to have Gretel whose medical expertise allowed her to brew a virus remedy concoction to immunize the masses. That immunization allows those of us who are inoculated to develop a natural immunity to the virus. A major comfort. Gretel thinks her potion might also protect us from any mutations of the virus. Another fear that the ambassador revealed to Gretel shortly before his death.

The wheel is bigger and grander than I remember. Or maybe it's that the farm is so quiet and seems so deserted.

I'm not sure about the future. How long can we hold them off? I fear that the Mercs will hear about our vaccine. I worry about the princess, the new prince, and the queen. I know that I will eventually have to try to save them.

I run my fingers over the rusted prongs of my wheel. I fall into the dilapidated chair. I set the ride on its lowest power. I decide not to think about it right now. For now, for today. I will ride my Ferris wheel basking in the love I witnessed today between my sister and my best friend. I will celebrate their marriage.

The wind blowing through my hair relaxes me. Serenity consumes me. Right this minute, all is right with my world.

Riding the Ferris wheel allows me to look out over the

farm. The harvests have been neglected. When this is all over, I'll need help to bring these crops back to life. It excites me to think about working the harvest again. To grow food for consumption by all of the people. How much more worthy of a profession is there than that? Maybe Riley would like to try farm life again after this is all over. A warm sensation tingles my senses.

At the top of this wheel, I spot a group of men riding horses onto the farm. This can't be. Who are they? Are they Mercs? How could the Mercs find us and why would they be out and about? Don't they think the virus is alive and well?

The men on the horses motion to those on the ground to gather. Are they arresting them? If so, I am caught now. I see Eddie and Baako being taken into the farm house. They don't seem to know the strangers. I know they were surprised. The children are huddled together and escorted in the house. The men stand beside their horses outside the house as if they are waiting on me to get off the wheel.

Who are these people? Are they going to kill me now? After all of this, why now? The minute I step off this wheel, I'm their prisoner.

I have no choice, it's not just about me. It's about Eddie, Baako, and the children. It's about all of us. I resign my thoughts. I'll do whatever I have to do to make sure they are all safe.

I grasp the four-leaf clover one last time as I come to the bottom of the Ferris wheel. I step out ready for whatever is coming next. I am willing to take my punishment.

Maybe I can talk myself out of this trouble too. Maybe I can save the others. I might get them to let the children go. All of these thoughts race through my mind all at once. One thing I know for sure, I won't give up. It's not in me. I'm a fighter. I'm a survivor.

I take a deep breath, shut down the wheel, jut my chin out, and walk defiantly to the group standing by their horses. I ready myself.

The leader turns around and faces me.

How can this be and what does this mean?

It is my father—the ambassador. Alive and well.
The big question is—whose side is he on?

Other Books By Susan Larned Womble

(Available on Amazon and Kindle)

1) **The Big Wheel** ISBN-13: 978-0-9913977-0-9
2) **Newt's World: Beginnings** ISBN: 978-0-9913977-1-6
3) **Newt's World: Internal Byte** ISBN: 978-0-9913977-2-3

4) **Newt's World: Beginnings Workbook Teacher's Edition** ISBN: 978-0-9913977-3-0

5) **Newt's World: Beginnings Workbook Student's Edition** ISBN: 978-0-9913977-4-7

6) **Newt's World: Internal Byte Workbook Teacher's Edition** ISBN: 978-0-9913977-5-4

7) **Newt's World: Internal Byte Workbook Student's Edition** ISBN: 978-0-9913977-6-1

Awards and Notables

- **Gold Medal Florida Book Award in children's literature 2008 for "Newt's World: Beginnings"**
- **Newt's World Beginnings on 2009, 2010, 2011, 2012, 2013, 2014 Just Read Florida Recommended Reading Lists**

Susan Larned Womble

ABOUT THE AUTHOR

Susan Womble is an award-winning author. Her first novel "Newt's World: Beginnings" won the 2008 Gold Medal Florida Book Award. "Newt's World: Beginnings" is also on the 2009-2014 Just Read Florida Recommended Reading List. Her writing credits also include "Newt's World Beginnings Workbook" (teacher's and student's editions), the second in the series entitled, "Newt's World: Internal Byte" and accompanying workbooks. Susan Womble lives in Tallahassee, Florida with her family. She is a National Board Certified teacher with a career of teaching grades K-12th in the areas of reading, special education, language arts, math, social studies, and the profoundly handicapped. While teaching overseas in Hohenfels, Germany, she traveled extensively throughout Europe. Her first series deals with issues she saw in her class. She looked at her students in her classroom and wrote her book with video gaming, computers, texting, technology, virtual worlds, bullying, cyberbullying, tolerance, and fitting in issues. Her book is a story of friendship. The hero Newt who uses a wheelchair discovers what friendship is about and how to deal with bullies. "The Big Wheel" and "Take the Helm" are dystopian stories. Womble decided to write about her experiences in Bavaria in these books using her firsthand accounts of the setting to weave a tale about a society long separated that has to find a way to work together again. Visit www.susanwomble.com for more information. Contact her at susan.womble@gmail.com.

Made in the USA
Charleston, SC
30 June 2014